Frank Midgette's Case
"The Dead Pan"

By Oliver Strong

Smashwords Edition

ISBN: 978-0-9575457-3-1

Word Count: 26,900

# CONTENTS

# Chapter One
## "I Walk The Line"

'The name's Frank, Frank Midgette, and just so you know that's pronounced Midg –ay, it's French.

When I was a wide eyed kid I thought I'd protect and serve. Thirty five years later I'm a homicide Lieutenant working out of Precinct 17, the shittiest job in the shittiest Precinct in the shittiest city ... God bless America!

Why am I telling you this? Well since I'm all alone, unless you count Johnny Cash and a bottle of cheap ass bourbon, I guess someone has to hear my eulogy before I blow my brains out ... damn that just made me think, better leave a few dollars for the cleaning lady. I bet that bitch charges extra for brains.'

Frank pulled a leather wallet from his jacket and put three $20 notes on the desk. He took another hit of bourbon as Johnny Cash sang "Cry, Cry, Cry" to a strumming guitar. The only object shinning inside that gloomy room was his pistol lying beside a half finished bottle. Its silvery steel captured on-lookers attention (not that there were any), the largest handgun in production a Smith & Wesson model 500, its shells almost twice the size of a Magnum 44.

Frank loaded a single round in the cylinder, spun it, upon coming to a halt he inserted its barrel in his mouth and pulled the trigger ... nothing ... damn he'd always been unlucky!

Frank took another slug of bourbon then another spin of the barrel ... damn ... maybe Jesus was trying to tell him something? Maybe he didn't like to see good booze go to waste, a sentiment Frank shared with the almighty.

Another shot of bourbon, if he kept going like this he'd finish the whole damn bottle, just the kind of shitty luck that plagued Frank for the last thirty five years, click ... damn, when the hell is this thing gonna work?

Frank's mobile phone went off, damn annoying contraptions but being a Homicide Detective he was required to carry one. Frank pulled the barrel out his mouth and fumbled through his jacket pockets until he got the mobile, 'Yeah, who the hell is it?'

'Good morning Lieutenant!' replied a female voice.

Frank made a grim sneer as he reached over and poured a drink, 'Morning Captain, this a business call, or your husband been caught picking up hookers again?'

'Funny Frank, finish your bourbon and report to me this morning, seven thirty sharp, you got it?'

'Sure, what's the occasion?'

'I've got a case that, well let's say it suits your special talents, see you in five hours.'

'Sure,' Frank turned off his police issue mobile took a momentary glance at his pistol, sighed and went for the booze whilst Johnny Cash sang the words to "Personal Jesus".


Eight thirty Frank pulled into Precinct 17 in his dirty Honda, slamming the door shut he stumbled inside.

'Morning Lieutenant,' called the staff Sergeant.

Frank shuffled over to him, 'You got a cigarette Pete?'

'I'm sorry sir, new regulations, we can't carry tobacco products you know that.'

'Don't give me that shit Pete I forgot mine.'

Pete looked around before taking out a packet of smokes and placing a few cigarettes into Frank's palm.

'Thanks.'

'No problem sir.'

Frank made his way upstairs, through offices, dressed in a crumpled grey suit he hadn't taken off in three days. At the far end someone pointed him out to a young lady, probably her first day; she trotted over and in a loud voice asked, 'Lieutenant Midget?'

The room went quiet and all eyes turned to the girl, 'That's Lieutenant Midg-ay ... it's French.'

'Oh I'm sorry.'

'What you want?'

'Captain Williams is waiting for you sir, it's very urgent.'

'Why, she got a pedicure booked in half an hour?'

The girl made and awkward expression, 'I erm, well.'

'Ah forget it kid.'

'Yes sir.'

Frank made his way to the back of the office floor and knocked the Captain's door, 'Come in.'

Frank stepped inside closing the door behind him.

Captain Jane Williams stood up, manicured hands pressed upon an oak desk, 'So you finally decided to make an appearance Lieutenant, I was wondering whether you or Michael Jackson would be the first to rise from his coffin ... you look like a bum that crawled out a whiskey bottle.'

Frank scratched his neck, straightened his collar then noticed a third person. A tall young Latino man, probably around thirty, dressed in a very dapper suit, 'Who the hell's this guy?'

'Lieutenant Manuel Montoya, meet Lieutenant Frank Midgette.'

Montoya offered his hand, 'Nice to meet you, sir.'

Frank laughed whilst shaking hands, 'Damn it son you smell like a whore house!'

Captain Williams smirked, 'Frank meet your new partner.'

Frank's demeanour changed rapidly as he withdrew his hand, 'Partner?'

'Why yes you've got a new case and Lieutenant Montoya here needs experience, you're going to teach him the trade.'

Frank shook his finger at Williams, 'Now listen here Captain I've taken a lot of shit but I ain't having Manolito as MY partner.'

Manuel's eyes widened.

'Calm down Frank, a new case a new partner it's exactly what you need to get back on your feet again.'

'Back on my feet? What the hell you talking about?'

'Come on Frank, it's hardly a secret you're on the edge.'

'On the edge of what?'

'Look at yourself, beggars in Commercial Park are classy compared to your sorry ass.'

'When was the last time you saw a beggar wearing a suit?' he pointed to his clothes.

'That isn't a suit it's a sleeping bag Frank.'

'Well maybe if I sucked my way up the ranks I'd be Captain of this Precinct and you'd be drinking bourbon alone every night!'

The Captain closed her eyes, gathering herself for a moment, 'Is that what you think Frank?'

'Damn right it is!'

'Captain of the shittiest Precinct in America along with a pension that probably won't be there on retirement, listening to your stinking ass bitch every day is poor compensation for sucking off the ugliest old men in the State.'

Manuel began to chuckle, distracting both Frank and the Captain from their bust up.

'Here's the case,' she held it out until he opened it.

Williams sat down to ogle her plaque, Captain Jane Williams Precinct 17 Detroit.

Frank spoke in an incredulous tone, 'You cannot be serious.'

'Is there a problem Lieutenant?'

'Some guy gets his nuts ripped off while taking a shit and you want me to investigate? I'm Homicide!'

Williams interlocked her fingers, 'He died, possibly murdered.'

'Oh please, he probably got his balls caught on the seat and stood up too fast.'

'The moment this case hit my desk it cried Frank Midgette, I just couldn't think of anyone who might have spent more time with their head down a public toilet.'

Manuel burst out laughing, Frank gave him a cold stare then turned to Williams, 'So why do I get to babysit Manolito?'

'His name is Lieutenant Manuel Montoya, I expect a preliminary report by tomorrow, you may leave now Lieutenant,' she motioned shooing him away.

As he opened the door several workmates scrambled back to their desks, having spent the last minutes with their ears against the Captain's door. Frank slammed the door shut displaying a dark look as he strode to the stairs. After Frank had left the young lady asked an old detective, 'Does everyone speak to the Captain like that?'

'Only Frank,' replied an old guy with a hefty beer gut.

'How come he gets away with it?'

'Frank doesn't speak nice to anyone but he brings the perps in … usually dead.'

'Oh.'


Manuel sat in the passenger seat of Frank's Honda, there was an awkward silence. Frank had the window down, one arm resting on the door, puffing smoke while Johnny Cash sang on his stereo.

'You know you don't have to call me Lieutenant.'

Frank grunted concentrating on the road ahead.

'You always so polite with the Captain?'

Frank gave another grunt then took a drag on his cigarette.

'You don't talk much … Lieutenant Midget.'

Frank braked hard in the middle of the road and glared at his partner, 'Now you listen to me spic, my name is Midg-ay, understood?'

'And my name is Manuel, understood?'

Road users tooted horns and shouted profanities whilst they exchanged gnarly looks.

'Fine,' said Frank.

'Fine,' replied Manuel.

Frank started his engine but before he could release the brake a car pulled up alongside with four black youths. A kid in the passenger seat shouted, 'Hey cracker! You put a dent on ma homeboy's new Benz, you gonna pay for it!'

Frank compared the class of vehicle to its occupants and came to a swift conclusion, 'You niggers steal a white man's car and want me to pay? You gotta be crazy!'

The youth produced a Mac 10 automatic weapon and replied in an angry voice, 'You gonna give me everything you got white boy!'

Feigning fear Frank's hands shook as he spoke in a shaky voice, 'Let me get my wallet, I've got four hundred in cash.'

'Quick cracker, before the cops get outta Dunkin Doughnuts.'

Frank moved a trembling hand inside his wrinkled jacket to producing a Smith & Wesson model 500. An expression of shock hit the youth moments before a titanic boom rang out causing the perp's head to explode. A bullet passed through the passenger's skull and into the driver's killing both, inside windows stained dark ruby red as thick blood sloshed in all directions re-painting its interior, rear passengers bailed drenched in gore and brains.

Frank opened his door jumped out and levelled his pistol, 'HALT!'

The youths turned to raise weapons, a pair of massive booms filled everyone's ears, when smoke cleared blood spattered over backed up traffic three cars down. Women screamed in terror, men lay in foetal positions praying to whatever deity they believed in today.

Frank called his partner, 'Hey,' he didn't respond, Frank shouted 'HEY!'

The young man was sitting in shock, his first day after being transferred from a good neighbourhood, never having fired a shot in anger or self-defence … one thing was sure … the price of laxatives were already rising in Manuel's neighbourhood.

'Hey, make yourself useful, call it in!'

As if in a trance his partner took the police radio, '10-52, four perps down, request assistance.'

Five minutes later three police cars appeared, sirens blaring, Frank stood on the pavement after purchasing a packet of cigarettes and a lighter from the local store. Whilst he puffed away Manuel remained ridged, not having moved an inch.

Regular police began taking witness statements, a senior police officer approached Lieutenant Midgette, 'Started early today Frank.'

'These damn niggers are getting more brazen, even Dracula was too frightened to come out in the day.'

'I guess so sir. I have to take your statement all the same, procedure.'

'Sure.'

After the Sergeant had taken Frank's statement an ambulance moved the bodies.

'So who's the guy with rigor mortis in your car?'

'My new partner.'

'Any good?'

'He called it in.'

'Four perps with three bullets, must be some sort of record.'

'The Captain's always bitching about efficiency, now she's got something to brag about the next time she has dinner with the Mayor,' Frank loaded three fresh rounds into the cylinder as the Sergeant raised his eyebrows.

Frank started his engine and began rolling down the road. Manuel didn't speak a word.

'You feeling hungry?' inquired Frank

Manuel said nothing.

'I could eat a horse, what you say we take a detour before investigating this stupid case?'

Manuel remained silent, staring ahead into nothingness.

Frank took a drag on his cigarette, 'You know I'm starting to like you ... Manuel.'

They pulled into the parking lot behind Annie's Diner, Frank coaxed Manuel inside. The pair sat down at the counter, a woman in her fifties approached, 'Morning Frank, anything new?'

'Nah, same old same old.'

'What you having?'

'Coffee and a hotdog with fries.'

'Your buddy?'

Frank prodded Manuel, 'What you having?'

He didn't say anything.

'What's wrong with him?' asked the lady.

'Got into one shoot out and the kid freezes up like Bill Clinton on a lie detector.'

'Geez, good job you had his back. Say, don't take this the wrong way Frank but the next time you come in here could you take a bath and shave first?'

'What's that supposed to mean?'

'Well you smell like my father's pants after he'd been out drinking with his friends, it's not good for customers.'

'Damn I got divorced so I didn't have to listen to this kind of shit every day.'

'She divorced you Frank, probably because you smell like a vagrant the neighbourhood cats use for a toilet.'

'Jesus, you and her related?'

'Just telling it how it is Frank and stop blaming your Captain, it isn't her fault she's younger, better looking and better qualified.'

'Don't get me started, you know the only reason she got that job is all this politically correct crap.'

'I'm not gonna argue about that, but she is younger and better looking.' Frank sneered, 'Does everyone get this abuse waiting for their food?'

'Oh no, you're a special case Frank, I wouldn't even consider extending it to regular customers.'

'Coffee, ma'am,' blurted Manuel.

Annie wrote it down, 'Anything else?'

He didn't speak.

'Get him some waffles, on me,' smiled Frank.

On delivery of their orders Frank tucked in, quickly putting away his breakfast and washing it down with coffee. After finishing his meal and on his third coffee he turned to see Manuel had barely touched his.

'Not hungry?'

'No.'

'Well finish your coffee I'll have Annie put that in a bag.'

Manuel nodded.

'What's up kid you couldn't stop talking earlier now it's like making conversation with Frankenstein's monster.'

Manuel peered at Frank, 'You killed four men.'

'It's like drinking your first whiskey, give it time and you'll get over it.'

Frank pulled a metal flask from inside his jacket flipped the top mixing some bourbon into his coffee. Holding it over Manuel's coffee he was about to pour before Manuel snatched his drink away, 'What the hell are doing?'

'What does it look like? I'm having my morning constitutional.'

'You can't drink on the job. You'll get dismissed for that.'

Annie raised an eyebrow.

'Loosen up kid, besides it keeps my hand steady, have some.'

'I don't drink, thank you Lieutenant.'

'Never mind, all the more for me,' Frank poured himself extra, he took a sip then pulled back his lips releasing a sigh of satisfaction, 'Aaahhhhh!'

'New day, new case, new partner … so far the only thing I got going for me is a hot dog, fries and some kick ass coffee. Manolito reminds of those people you see walking the streets or having dinner in a trance tapping on those smart phone things. You ever notice that, someone having dinner with a hot piece of ass and he's more concerned about discussing gay rights over twitter? Something's gotta be wrong there.

The case has gotta be Williams' idea of a joke, probably what she gets off on nowadays, now that she's riding a desk and half the city council … dirty bitch.

This morning … what can I say … it's the middle of summer so it's hot, as hot as Hilary Clinton's email account.'

# Chapter Two
## "Hard Day Blues"

'It was a hot day, the whole city was like a bitch on heat, I had to investigate the dumbest case ever and at the same time break in a rookie. It was downtown in a blues club, this guy named Stones had lost his nuts sack while taking a shit earlier this morning, ironic right?
The Captain didn't take this case seriously, how could she? So she didn't take me seriously and this was another crappy case in a long line of crappy cases until I got pissed off and collected my pension.
What about my new partner? Manuel Montoya, there was at least one thing in his favour, he didn't get in the way, could've been worse, I might've been stuck with some spic who thinks he's a real piece of hot shit.
I had my breakfast so now it was time to check the toilets and get this case over with. I bet that bitch is sitting in her chair laughing about it to the Chief right now.'

Frank pulled up outside a club "The Black Light", he and Manuel walked through the main entrance. A chubby black guy leant against the bar dressed in a very nice suit and hat, 'You Homicide?'
'Sure,' replied Frank, 'how'd you guess?'
'We don't get too many white folks in here, second when we do get white folks it's usually to arrest black folks.'
Frank lit up a cigarette, 'Damn I'm starting to like this shit hole already, you got any peanuts, you know the real salty ones?'
'Who the hell you think you are? I ain't giving no free shit to a cracker cop, you want something you can pay for it.'
'Fine, where's the scene?'
'This way,' the owner led them past two police officers into the public toilets. Inside another officer opened a cubicle but there was no white outline where a dead body should have fallen. Frank opened his case document, flicked through until discovering a photograph. A was sat up on the toilet, pants around ankles, ridged with a look of horror.
Manuel looked over Frank's shoulder then whipped out his note book, 'May I have your name sir?'
'Lebron Montel.'

Frank chuckled to himself causing offence to the owner.

'Hey you think something's funny cracker?'

'I don't understand why you niggers can't speak good English since you all play scrabble.'

'Say what cracker?'

'When it comes time to naming kids I'm certain you niggers just grab a bunch of scrabble letters then make a name out of whatever you get.'

'I oughta kick your damn ass outta here cracker!'

'If you did that your club wouldn't be opening for a long time … Lebron.'

'So I gotta take this abuse?' he glared at Manuel, 'This cracker talk to you like that bro?'

Frank intervened, 'He's just here to take notes they leave the thinking to white folks, like when to allow blues clubs to reopen.'

'Come on the guy had his nut sack ripped off, no-one saw nothing I've told you and about twenty witnesses so why I gotta go through this bullshit again?'

'My Captain thinks it might be a murder.'

'Murder? Listen no guy's gonna kill another guy by ripping off his nut sack, it just goes without saying.'

'According to reports the scrotum wasn't recovered.'

'Scrotum?'

'That's English for nut sack.'

'Oh, yeh like I said no-one went in before him, security cameras confirmed it.'

'It says here he was inside for thirty minutes, thirty minutes and no-one took a piss in this joint?'

'The band was playing their set, probably why no-one heard him scream.'

'How'd you know he screamed.'

Lebron gave Frank a coy stare over his stylish purple shades.

'Was the door open?'

Lebron thought for a second, 'Yeh you know it was, maybe he forgot to lock it?'

Frank looked around a bloody pan, 'Is that when you called the police?'

'Yeh, we didn't touch nothing.'

'Did you flush the toilet at any point?'

'Nope.'

'Strange.'

'What?'

'Ah, could be nothing, have you seen this guy either in or out of your club before this incident?'

'Never seen the cat before.'

'You getting this Lieutenant Montoya?'

'Yes sir.'

'Good, I'll be checking your notes.'

Frank examined the door lock it was in perfect working order, he went over the inside of the door searching for something.

'What you doin' cracker?'

'Looking to see if the door was forced from the inside but it's clean and since there're no marks on the outside, I don't understand.'

'Don't understand what?'

'Assuming he didn't tear off his own scrotum then wait to bleed to death, someone else did it. But they had to get inside the cubicle to commit the assault.'

'Like I said maybe he forgot to lock the door?'

Frank tapped his box of smokes, took a cigarette and lit it up.

'Hey, there's no smokin' in here cracker.'

'There's no castration either.'

Lebron gave an annoyed expression as Frank took a drag and contemplated the dilemma.

'So either the door was open or someone requested he open it, the only other possibility is the perpetrator was already in the cubicle when he entered.'

'Hey this ain't no faggot club,' stated Lebron.

'What if his attacker climbed over the cubicle wall?' conjected Manuel.

Frank replied with a withering expression, 'If you were taking a shit and I started climbing in you'd pull up your pants and get the hell outta there.'

'What if I had a gun?'

'Why the fuck would you be climbing a shithouse wall if you had a gun? You'd wait until I'd finished then hold me up. Besides look at the ceiling, there ain't enough clearance for a grown man to climb the wall.'

'Maybe he held him up, cut off the victim's scrotum leaving him sitting on the toilet; it'd account for the door and seemingly no sign of a struggle except a little blood spatter.'

'Fine, so let's say you're right and I was the attacker and I wanted to kill the victim in a certain way, why the hell would I select the bathroom of this establishment?'

Manuel and Lebron shrugged.

'It makes no sense to take that extra risk, unless I had no other opportunity.'

'So who's the cat with his nuts cut off?' inquired Lebron.

'His nuts were physically torn off according to the coroner and his name was Demetrius Stones.'

Lebron grimaced, 'Sounds like he had it coming.'

'According to this report he'd not yet defecated.'

'Defe what?'

'That means shit to you.'

'I guess his asshole tightened up when he felt a hand around his nuts?'

Frank walked out to the bar and sat down, 'You got bourbon?'

'Hey I don't sell durin' the day.'

'You ain't selling.'

Manuel spoke in a concerned tone, 'Sir you've already had one drink if the Captain found out.'

'To hell with the Captain, she's too busy getting a manicure to give a shit about us, sit down, take it easy.'

Lebron poured two shots and placed a bowl of peanuts on the bar, 'So are you gonna let me open tonight?'

'The question, Lebron, is what's it worth to you?' Frank knocked his shot down as Manuel observed wide eyed.

'You trying to blackmail me?' said Lebron in an incredulous tone.

Frank took a handful of peanuts, 'No Lebron I AM blackmailing you, now tell me, how much cash you got in your office safe?'

'I don't know what you talking about cracker.'

Frank smiled as he crunched on peanuts.

'Come on bro I gotta make a living.'

'Gone from cracker to bro in five seconds, must be a lot of cash in that safe Lebron.'

'Two hundred bucks,' said the owner with a steely gaze.

Frank chuckled, 'Two hundred bucks, what do you think I am some dumb ass rookie?'

'Three hundred.'

'I'll take four hundred.'

'Bro! That's my profit in one night!'

'Four hundred bucks Lebron, you still have to pay wages, rent and utilities while those doors are shut for the next two weeks.'

'TWO WEEKS!'

Frank raised his shot glass, 'Another bourbon … bro.'

Lebron poured a second drink before disappearing behind the bar into his office. Lebron opened his safe and counted out four hundred bucks, stopping for a moment he examined a loaded pistol kept inside just in case he was forced to open it by robbers. Lebron decided a shootout over four hundred dollars wasn't worth the risk, besides win or lose he'd lose. The porky owner returned cash in hand, 'Here take it you filthy bastard.'

'Thank you Mr Montel,' Frank folded the cash and slipped it inside his jacket, 'you play any Johnny Cash in this establishment?'

Lebron sneered, 'This ain't no honkytonk, that cat died listening to the blues baby, the only way to go in my opinion.'

'The band was playing live?'

'They played for half an hour.'

'Maybe he got depressed and ripped his own nuts off?'

'Then why come to a blues club?'

Frank's mobile rang, damn thing was always bothering him, 'Yeh, Lieutenant Midgette.'

'There's been another murder Frank, downtown at the Penobscot building. It's not in our jurisdiction but the Mexican Consulate died under similar conditions.'

Frank took a hit of bourbon, 'Sure thing, I'll finish up here and be on my way.'

'Are you drinking again Frank?'

'Just getting my mojo workin' Captain.'

'Jesus Christ Frank the press is at the Penobscot building, don't mention this case and whatever you do don't breathe near them, understood?'

'Gotcha Captain,' Frank put his mobile away, 'Manolito, looks like we got another missing nut sack, drink up.'

Manuel glared at his shot glass, 'I don't drink on duty.'

Frank reached over and threw the spirit down his neck, 'Ahhh, I'll make a call to the station; you can open tonight Lebron.'

'Gee thanks officer I don't know what I'd do without you.'

Frank picked his cigarette out the ashtray and exited the club. Once inside the old Honda and on their way to Detroit's financial district Manuel shook his head, 'I can't believe what you did back there, we're supposed to protect and serve not blackmail and extort.'

Frank looked at the road ahead one hand on the wheel the other on his cigarette as Johnny Cash played one of his hits, 'That wasn't blackmail, his club would've been closed for at least a week. I got it open for tonight, saved that poor bastard a lot more than four hundred dollars.'

'Is that how you justify extortion? Come on man don't give me that crap.'
Frank blew smoke out the car window stopping at a red light; he pulled the bribe from inside his jacket and counted out two one hundred dollars, 'Fine I'll split it.'
Manuel was shocked, 'I don't want your dirty money!'
Frank put the cash back as the light turned green, 'Don't be so naïve kid, everyone's on the take in that Precinct.'
'That's bullshit!'
'Listen Manolito, I know you spent your time on the force in some nice upper middle class district. Good people, low crime, no niggers, no spics, no white trash. You probably never fired a shot outside the range and the toughest decision you ever made was whether to have sprinkles on your doughnut today.'
Manuel was angry yet he didn't deny Frank's accusation.
'Well life's different on the other side of the tracks, we get paid less for longer hours, there's every type of low life ready to put a bullet in your back and yeah I take cash on the side, it's called danger money.
I know you're gonna report me to the Captain but my advice is don't bother.'
'Why?'
Frank chuckled as he took another drag, 'That dirty bitch would make Bernie Madoff a saint in comparison.'
Manuel pressed his lips tightly together and glared ahead.
Frank rested an arm on the car door, 'Don't believe me do you kid?'
Manuel refused to speak.
'If you reported me for drinking on the job and extortion back in good town they'd launch a full investigation and discipline me, right?'
'Discipline? You'd be dishonourably discharged then sent to prison!'
It was quiet for about twenty seconds.
'So how come you got transferred from Grosse Pointe to Mckinley street?'
'I didn't feel I was doing enough to help people, thought I could do some good in the rougher neighbourhoods.'
Frank laughed, 'Damn kid you're one of those naïve idealists.'
'So what are you Frank?'
Frank stopped chuckling, 'I was like you kid.'
'And then?'
'And then I grew up, found the world doesn't work that way.'
'I have to disagree on that.'

'Maybe in Grosse Pointe but where you work today, the world where all the niggers, spics and white trash live it doesn't work that way and since you decided to make it your quest to help them I gotta teach you how it is on the other side of the tracks before they kill you. So you tell the Captain what you saw today and see what happens, it'll be your first lesson on how it goes down at Precinct 17.'

Manuel leant over and whispered, 'Fine.'

'Damn stupid kid, got a wife and daughter living in a great neighbourhood, working the easiest job in Detroit. I mean come on, a Homicide Detective in Grosse Pointe? That's like being a Viagra salesman at the playboy mansion … maybe that wasn't the best analogy but you get what I'm saying. The kid had it easy his parents probably worked their asses off getting there, next thing they know he's transferring back to the ghetto, dumb ass kid.

The city was roasting by now, Manolito was practically on fire, he couldn't wait to report me. It brought a smile to my face, if only I could be a fly on the wall when that bitch tells him to keep his mouth shut. Ah yeh baby, good old Captain Jane Williams. She used to be my partner … not that kind of partner I mean we worked together in Homicide. Political correctness working its wonderful magic again, seems it always finds its way to me. She was as dirty as they came, the old Captain was on his last legs, stress, a bad heart and a divorce, it was only a matter of time before he retired or God retired him; and Lieutenant Jane Williams was there to help him on his way. I always wondered if she was sucking him off while he wrote that recommendation. I mean how the hell does she get to be Captain after I worked my ass off for thirty years, and Mike was supposed to be my friend, ah what am I saying, stupid bastard could never resist the women … and maybe it had something to do with that time he came home early and found me screwing his wife when I was supposed to be on duty? Some people can't help but hold a grudge …'

# Chapter Three
## "Big River"

'I pulled up in front of the Penobscot building, the centre of finance in this turd of a city circling the crap hole of America; Another bourbon would be pretty sweet right now, as for Manolito he was itching to tell tales to the Captain and get me fired, hah, there's an old saying in Precinct 17 … you're only naïve once.

The press are outside hunting a story, swarming around an ambulance whilst a ring of cops hold them back. I get out the car to be greeted by a couple of homicide detectives, a pair of assholes begging for a bullet in the back of their heads … boy if only it was them who'd transferred to Precinct 17.'

Two men dressed in very smart civilian suits obviously costing more than Frank's last three pay cheques smirked as he approached.

'Afternoon Frank, what you doing out in the daylight, got tired staring at the underside of the same rock?' shouted a detective. His partner, a guy in his mid-thirties, chuckled like an adolescent schoolboy.

'I was on my way to see your wife Gonzalez but this got called in, seems she's not the only spic in town who needs a hard examination,' stated Frank with an absolutely straight face.

Gonzalez lost his humorous demeanour, 'You watch your mouth Midget or I'm likely to crack you one, press or no press.'

His younger partner grabbed his arm restraining Gonzalez. Manuel was confused as to what exactly the beef was between these two.

'So why don't you tell me about this case instead of screwing around?' Gonzalez sneered, produced his note book, just before he spoke Frank whispered, 'And it's Midg-ay.'

Gonzalez continued with his report, 'The Mexican Consulate was found dead this morning, Esteban Rivera. His secretary discovered him, sitting on the toilet, pants around his ankles, scrotum missing, seemingly torn off with violent force … what a way to go!'

'How long had he been there?'

'The doc says an hour or so.'

'Where's the body?'

'Oh he's still on the throne, awaiting your distinguished presence.'

Frank took out his smokes, tapped the carton, a Camel slid out, he lit it up then turned to Gonzalez after taking a deep drag, 'Why don't you do me a favour Miguel, call your wife and tell her I'll be late today.'

'FUCK YOU MIDGET!' screamed Lieutenant Gonzalez as Frank and Manuel climbed inside the police cordon.

They reached the elevator within a large atrium, displaying badges men in blue parted allowing them to ascend the old gothic building. Manuel shook his head whilst giving Frank a disappointed stare.

'What's troubling your ass kid?'

'You've just got this way with people ain't you Frank?'

Frank cackled as he puffed his cigarette.

'Everyone I meet either hates your guts or hasn't met you yet. You should treat other Officers of the law with the greatest respect.'

'They teach you that at Pointe Grosse?'

'They did as a matter of fact.'

Frank cackled again, 'What'd they say about their wives?'

'I thought you hated blacks and hispanics.'

'I can see you've never had the acquaintance of Mrs Gonzalez, you should pay her a visit son.'

'Thanks but no thanks.'

As the elevator moved upwards Frank couldn't stop himself from laughing, 'She's screwed her way through all nine districts, why not?'

'I'm a happily married man, thank you.'

'Happily married, that's an oxymoron if ever I heard one.'

'Who taught you that?'

'My bitch ex-wife.'

The doors opened to more cops, Frank and Manuel displayed their badges and were led to suite 830. They observed a fine office of mahogany and old leather, 'He's in here Lieutenant.'

A doctor and three medics waited to remove the body and transport it. Frank opened the door to a small en suite bathroom, inside the Mexican consulate sat on the toilet, pants around his ankles and an excruciating expression. The first thing Frank observed were the plush surroundings, polished brass and white marble, very decadent, 'Nice digs.'

The next observation he made was an iPod, the consulate still had its earphones inserted like a pair of plugs. Frank delicately removed the device then rummaged through the former Consulate's expensive suit. He found a wallet, opened it and read the driver's license, 'Esteban Rivera, poor bastard.'

Manuel asked the doctor, 'Did you find his scrotum?'

'Nope, seems he may have flushed it away.'

Frank turned to the doctor, 'Why do you say that?'

'Well who else could have done it?'

'What do you mean?'

'I'm sorry Lieutenant I didn't mean to impose.'

'No go on.'

'I just heard the police officers taking witness reports, they said CCTV recorded no-one other than the Consulate enter or leave his office the whole time, oh except his secretary, she found him.'

Frank scratched his head, 'Thanks, where's the secretary?'

'She's in the office Lieutenant.'

Frank moved back into the office to meet an attractive young lady in her mid-twenties with a pair of thick rimmed glasses, 'Hello Miss?'

'Miss Ramos.'

'Hi, I'm Lieutenant Midgette, this is Lieutenant Montoya we're here to investigate any possibility of foul play.'

She shook his hand, 'Hello.'

Frank gave her a seedy look, 'So Miss Ramos, what were you doing in the Consulate's bathroom?'

'I had some documents that required his signature.'

'What documents?'

The girl looked decidedly uncomfortable, 'Erm they were about visa applications.'

'Whose visas?'

'Americans holidaying in Mexico.'

'When did the consulate enter his office?'

'Oh he always got to work early about six in the morning.'

Manuel noted her testimony, 'When did you start work today Miss?'

She replied in an awkward tone, 'I was here at six thirty.'

'The Consulate opens at eight o'clock, am I right?'

The girl blushed as Frank grinned.

'That's correct officer,' responded Miss Ramos.

'Did you see anyone enter or leave the Consulate's office during that time?'

'No, you see I work just outside his office and I'd have seen anyone coming in or out.'

'Were you at your post all this time?'

The girls face went red and Frank cut in, 'Never mind we got the CCTV footage, apparently it confirms your story Miss Ramos. It seems you were the only one to enter and leave his office during the time he was alive. So tell me, did you hear anything?'

'No, the walls and the doors are very thick.'

Frank noted the old oak doors on both the entrance to the office and bathroom, 'So what time did you discover his body?'

'Ten fifty, we were about to close for lunch, I brought some paperwork for Esteban to sign and he wasn't in his office. I waited then checked his bathroom and found him … dead,' the girl was obviously shook up, she began to fall apart in tears.

'The door was open?'

'Yes officer.'

'You can go now Miss Ramos,' Frank examined the iPod as the young lady left.

Manuel whispered, 'I'm certain she was hiding something.'

'Sure she was, Esteban was knocking the bottom out that dirty bitch every morning and during the lunch break,' smirked Frank.

'You've got a filthy mind Frank.'

'She wasn't hiding anything more than a good hard banging at breakfast followed by a blow job for lunch. Damn I should've been a Consulate, start work at eight, three hours later take an hour for lunch then close shop by one in the afternoon. Get paid a fortune for knocking the bottom out some young girl before going home to the wife.'

Manuel shook his head, 'So what do you think about this death Frank?'

Frank took a drag on his smoke, 'Same as before, the door was open with no obvious sign of a struggle. CCTV confirms her story; no-one went in or out other than her and the victim.'

'So she did it, right?'

Frank chuckled to himself, 'And then called the police, after killing him in the Mexican Consulate covered by CCTV twenty four hours a day?'

'Maybe they were having sexual relations and he dumped her or refused to leave his wife, a crime of passion?'

'Just after she'd got back from Lebron's club and washed her hands, right?'

'Coincidence.'

'There's no such thing as coincidence, not when you work in homicide kid.'

'So if it wasn't her then he did it to himself.'

'Two men committed suicide in the same freaky manner within twelve hours, another coincidence I don't believe in kid.'

'So what do you think Frank?' he asked in a tired tone.

'I think he's the unluckiest Mexican in the United States.'

'How's that?'

'Think about it, he didn't cross the border by swimming over a river then outrunning packs of dogs. He gets a good paying job with ridiculously easy hours and great pussy. He had it all then someone rips his balls off while taking a shit.'

'Jealous wife?'

'No-one went in or out, the girl didn't do it, he didn't do it and it confirms what that shifty bastard Lebron said,' Frank turned to the doctor, 'OK you can take Mr Rivera away.'

As the medics wrapped it up Frank watched a moustachioed expression of horror disappear behind a body bag before being carted off. He then took out the Consulates wallet and removed its remaining cash.

'What you doing Frank, that's stealing from the dead!' whispered Manuel.

'Then he ain't gonna miss it. There's seven hundred dollars, you want three?'

'No way!'

'Fine I'll give you four.'

'Frank I'm reporting this you know.'

'Yeh, yeh, yeh, you be a good boy and tell Williams.'

'I'm not joking Frank.'

Frank took the Consulate's cash then his iPod, put the earphones on and played the last tune. The next thing Frank heard was Muddy Waters singing "Got my mojo workin'", 'I think we got everything here, let's get back to the Precinct. I can take a look at the CCTV footage and you can tell tales to the Captain.'


Back in Precinct 17 Manuel went straight to Captain William's office, inside he chronicled Frank Midgette's racist abuse, sexism, extortion, drinking on the job and stealing from a dead Mexican.

Captain Jane Williams removed her glasses and looked up from a police report, 'Thank you for bringing this to light Lieutenant Montoya, I'll be sure to have a talk with Lieutenant Midgette. You may return to your duties now.'

Manuel pulled a puzzled expression, 'Captain, I request to be reassigned.'

'Request denied you'll stay assigned to Lieutenant Midgette.'

'But ...'

'There are no ifs and buts in Precinct 17 Lieutenant, you get an assignment and I expect you to fulfil it, understood?'

'To be honest, no, I don't understand.'

Williams sighed, leaning back into her leather seat, 'You say he made racist comments you found offensive?'

'Yes sir.'

'My advice is learn to be a big boy and suck it up Lieutenant.'

'What about extorting Mr Lebron Montel this morning, should he suck it up?'

'The cost of doing business in Detroit Lieutenant.'

'Isn't that what taxes are for, sir.'

Williams shook her head, 'You think that bastard pays his taxes? I've had the Chief on my ass because the Mayor's on his ass because people like Lebron aren't paying their taxes and therefore Precinct 17 gets less funding than any precinct in Detroit!'

'Drinking while on duty?'

'After taking down four perps this morning the man deserves a drink, and according to reports you were frozen in fear while Frank covered YOUR ASS, if anyone should be under investigation it should be you Lieutenant. You're lucky Frank hasn't come down here to complain about your performance today because if he did I'd have you busted back to Pointe Grosse in a cold second.'

Manuel began to sweat under the fierce fire of his new Captain's barbecue, 'Stealing money out of the Mexican Consulate's wallet?'

Williams interlocked her fingers, 'Are you serious?'

'Yes I am sir.'

'Well when Mr Esteban Rivera puts in a request for the return of his allegedly ...'

'Allegedly?'

'Allegedly,' replied Williams in a forceful voice, 'missing cash, I'll look into it.'

'Sexism?'

She chuckled, 'I worked the beat with that asshole for ten years Lieutenant, get over it!'

'Is that it Captain?'

'One last piece of advice Lieutenant, Frank Midgette is the lowest dirtiest drunken piece of crap in this sorry Precinct, but he taught me everything I know about policing. So instead of bitching listen and learn, goodbye Lieutenant please close the door behind you.'

Manual exited the Captain's office in shock, as he opened the door workmates scarpered back to their seats, pretending they hadn't eves dropped a moment ago. He walked in a trance to join his partner who was going over CCTV footage from Lebron's and the Consulate.

He got to the lab, Frank was chatting with a lady recently assigned to Precinct 17. The conversation had moved from his case to dinner, unfortunately she wasn't particularly attracted by the odour of bourbon and cigarettes. She walked away whilst Frank eyed her behind with that leer only Frank could produce around decent folk.

'You done Frank?'

'I wish … sorry … so what'd the Captain tell you?'

'She told me to suck it up.'

'Anything else?'

'That you're a piece of shit but a good cop.'

Frank raised an eye, 'She said I was a good cop?'

'Yeh.'

'Well I looked the footage over, it all checks out; seems these guys were killed by someone who got in and out without being detected.'

There was no way to get in and out of that Consulate without being detected, you might trick the CCTV or the secretary but you ain't gonna trick them both at the same time.

Frank tapped his cigarette carton then lit up a smoke, 'Unless you don't.'

'Don't what?'

'Trick the CCTV and secretary, there must be another way in and out.'

Manuel gave a big huff, 'So how are we supposed to work it out?'

Frank took a long drag on his smoke, 'Find the scrotum then we can work out how the perp got in and out.'

'How the hell do we do that Frank?'

'If you'd cut off his nut sack how would you dispose of it?'

'Flush it.'

'That's what I was thinking kid, and where's the closest toilet?'

Manuel smiled, 'So we get someone who knows the sewers to check it out.'

Frank grinned whilst puffing on his smoke, 'Good thinking kid.'

'Damn, it's only afternoon and I got a wetback with a wet ass and no ball sack. The slut he was knocking off is more worried about losing her career than him losing his life, and people call me cynical when I say love is dead? Still I got seven hundred bucks out of it and a free iPod, gotta say he had good taste in women and music.

Did I say the city was hot? Yeh, well it slipped my mind after going over the footage, heh, gotta admit I was examining the new girl's tits too. I guess she doesn't go for the older more dignified type but I tell you this, if Manolito hadn't interrupted I'd have had her skirt up and ankles behind her ears. Maybe I'll take a visit to the lab when that kid's off duty.

I don't know why I'm thinking about this shit, I gotta case to solve. The guys in the office reckon since Dirty Harry had the dead pool I ought to get "The Dead Pan" ... yeh real funny right? The Captain's probably told the Chief and he's told the Mayor, I bet those assholes are laughing about me over salmon and Champagne while I search for nuts!'

# Chapter Four
## "I've Been Everywhere"

'I said the city was hot, well it stank too, me and Manolito were headed down the city sewers. Some guy named Rod got us all kitted out in suits before descending the depths.
Damn … I'd woken up in some shitty dives stinking like a dead dog's ass but this was something else. Walking in tunnels flowing with crap, everyone's shit rich man and poor's alike and I thought I had a dirty job. Manolito's holding a handkerchief over his nose and mouth like he's royalty or something. You'd think he's never smelt an asshole in his life, I smell one every time I walk into the Precinct, the kid'll get used to it. As for Rod he can't stop yammering about his job and how tough it is, I'm starting to have flash backs to my ex-wife. Funny how the aroma of shit combined with an unrelenting droning noise ignites certain memories. I bet that bitch would've ripped off my nut sack given half the chance.'

Frank lit up a cigarette hoping to remove the stench of excrement from his nostrils. Manuel started to regret he wasn't a smoker himself.
'We're not allowed to smoke down here Lieutenant,' stated the short worker.
'It's the only way I can get that stink out my nose,' replied Frank.
'Ah you get used to it after a few months in waste management.'
Frank gave a disparaging grunt, 'Is that what they call it these days?'
Rod stopped, 'My official title is Waste Water Manager, so please refer to me as such.'
'Did they put any extra zeros on your paycheque when they added those extra letters?'
Rod carried on, he refrained from chattering anymore. Finally they reached a pipe leading away from the Penobscot building, 'Well here it is boys.'
'What now?' inquired Manuel.
Rod grinned, 'It's time for you to get down and dirty.'
'Ain't you gonna help?'
Rod laughed sarcastically, 'I'm sorry but they didn't add enough zeros to my paycheque.'

Manuel gave Frank a black look, 'Good job Frank if you got any more put downs keep it to yourself.'

Frank and Manuel donned rubber gloves and shone flashlights while sifting through the cities shit.

'If it came from the Penobscot building it could be anywhere down there,' Rod pointed all the way down the sewer, 'but tell me what you're looking for and when it was flushed, I reckon I could narrow it down.'

Frank flicked his cigarette into a stream of piss and shit, 'A guy lost his scrotum, had it ripped off balls and all, got flushed sometime around ten this morning.'

'I see then we should move about two hundred feet down, you won't find anything from this morning here.'

Manuel wiped urine and excrement from his gloves, 'Thanks.'

'So someone got their scrotum cut off and flushed it?'

'It was torn off,' noted Manuel.

'Ouch!' Rod giggled, 'I bet that made his eyes water.'

'Probably.'

'So who did it, the wife?'

'We don't know right now.'

'What do you mean you don't know, didn't you ask him?'

Frank cut in, 'Nope.'

'Why not?'

'First lesson in Homicide you want a statement from a corpse … ask the coroner.'

Rod went pale as he considered the horrible method by which this fellow had passed away, 'It should be just up here.'

After twenty minutes of searching with hands and flashlights they found it. Lying on the edge of a river of piss sat a white scrotum void of colour due to blood loss.

'Bag it,' stated Frank.

Manuel grimaced, 'Why don't you bag it Frank?'

'Because I'm the big cheese and this is your first day on the job, so bag it.'

'Great, my first day and I'm in the city sewer bagging some guy's scrotum. You know this job's a lot more glamorous on TV Frank.'

'Hmm, that's strange,' stated Rod.

'What's that?' replied Frank as Manuel placed the item in a plastic evidence bag.

'You say it was about ten o'clock?'

'Yeh.'

'It doesn't make sense that it got all this way down the pipe yet there's no discolouring.'

'I don't understand.'

'Well look how far it came,' he pointed to where they'd come from, 'that's a lot of waste to get dragged through, right?'

'Sure.'

Rod pointed at the dismembered scrotum, 'So how come that's not picked any of it up,' Rod paused for a moment, 'LOOK!'

Frank couldn't believe his eyes, not far away lay a second and a third scrotum both removed in the same fashion and bearing very little in the way of stains or marks after journeying through a river of human waste, 'Manolito, bag 'em.'

Manuel pulled out two more evidence bags and got to work.

Frank went to grab a smoke but realised his cigarettes rested inside his biohazard suit, 'Let's get out of here, I've gotta think this over.'

Topside they removed their suits and Frank lit up a smoke, 'You say it's not possible for those scrotums to get that far down the pipe or be that long in the sewer without getting dirty?'

'Yup,' replied Rod.

'Would you give Lieutenant Montoya a statement to that effect?'

'Sure.'

After taking the Waste Manager's statement the pair got into Frank's Honda and returned to the Precinct. They moved through the office on their way upstairs to hand in the evidence. A cry went out from another officer, 'Hey Frank you stink of shit and got some dude's nuts in your hand again?'

A ripple of laughter rang around the office, Captain Williams stepped out and it went quiet. She held onto a file with both hands, raising her eyebrow at Frank.

Frank peered at her then back toward his workmate, 'Sure thing Grady, I found them in your momma's bedroom slapping against her skanky ass!'

The room erupted, O'Grady marched towards Frank, the man was furious. He took a swing, Frank blocked it and delivered a jab to O'Grady's face leaving the fellow in confusion. Frank kneed his opponent in the groin much to the audience's satisfaction, just as he was to finish O'Grady with a hard cross Captain Williams shouted over the ruckus, 'ENOUGH!'

Frank stopped, O'Grady crumpled to his knees wincing in pain, hands around his private parts, 'Get back to work, and Frank I want your nuts in the lab ASAP!'

Frank and Manuel made their way up stairs where evidence was held and examined. Manuel shook his head, 'Did it again didn't you Frank.'
'Did what?'
'Unleashed that je ne sais quoi.'
'Je ne sais what?'
Manuel gave a coy look, 'It's French Frank.'
'Bah, Grady's a pencil pushing asshole, the Captain's had him riding a desk for a year after that shootout on Grand River Avenue.'
'What happened?'
'Some perps held up a gas station, he got stage fright, was lucky to make it out alive, ever since he's been in deep freeze.'
'Deep freeze?'
'Personnel, riding a desk until he takes a pension just he's too damn stubborn.'
They reached the top floor, turned down a corridor and pushed through a set of heavy steel doors, a placard stated Peter Hertz MD. A white haired Doctor looked over his glasses, 'Hi there Frank, how's it going?'
'Same shit, different day.'
'I heard about the shoot out today, nice to see you haven't lost your touch.'
'News travels fast doc.'
'Added to that I had four bodies on the slab with only three shots fired I knew right then it could only be Frank Midgette.'
Frank chuckled then gestured towards Manuel, 'I got something for you to examine.'
Manuel handed over three bags each containing a victim's scrotum.
Hertz looked him up and down, 'This your new partner Frank?'
'The Captain's idea.'
'I see ... they're already taking bets you know?'
'What's it looking like?'
'Ten days three to one, I was going to ask you before I placed my bet.'
'Say what?' blurted Manuel.
Frank scratched his chin, 'What's the odds on fourteen days?'
The Doctor had a deadly serious expression on his face, 'That's running at ten to one.'
'Any higher?'
'Bradley's offering twenty to one if he makes it past twenty days.'
'He can back it up?'
The Doctor nodded his head.

Manuel's expression met somewhere between utter disgust and total shock.

Frank pointed at the Doctor, 'Put me down for five hundred.'

Hertz replied in a very concerned tone, 'Are you sure Frank?'

Midgette pulled five hundred of the seven hundred dollars donated by the Mexican Consulate, 'Take it.'

Doctor Hertz whipped the money out of Frank's hands and began to count the notes; next he moved to a microscope.

'What the hell's going on here?' yelped Manuel.

'Shut up kid,' stated Frank.

Doctor Hertz finished his examination of all five notes, 'Looks legit this time Frank.'

'That wasn't my fault.'

'Frank you busted him for counterfeiting.'

'It wasn't intentional you know that.'

'Sure Frank, I'm certain you won't take any offence when I verify your good intentions from now on.'

Manuel broke up the conversation again, 'I'm sorry to interrupt this but what exactly are you two wagering on?'

Hertz folded the money up and placed it in his breast pocket, 'You of course.'

'Might you expand a little on that Doctor?'

'Your life expectancy to be exact, the record for Frank's partner is held by the Captain in fact she's the only one that's still alive. The previous seventeen died on duty.'

'So how long did the last one live?'

'Six days, you owe me a hundred bucks on that Frank.'

Frank groaned, 'I swear I'll pay you back doc.'

Manuel shook his head in disbelief, 'Does the Captain know about this?'

'Sure,' stated the Doctor in a rather surprised tone, 'she's got two hundred at three to one.'

'Well I must say I'm flattered!'

'You should be kid, the last one she bet fifty and that was only five days.'

Frank patted Manuel on the back, 'Don't sweat it kid.'

'Sweat it? I got my own Captain betting I'm gonna get wasted in ten days!'

'Nine days,' interrupted the Doctor.

'What?'

'Nine days, this would be the first day, she's betting on the tenth day not in ten days.'

'Oh I do apologise!'

'Look don't take it the wrong way I'm quite certain Frank will look after you.'

'Like the other seventeen suckers? How do I know they didn't get wasted by someone in this Precinct?'

The Doctor put his hands in his pockets and there was an awkward silence for ten seconds.

Manuel smiled, 'No, no, no, you guys are just yanking my chain, yeh that was a good one fellas you had me going for a moment.'

The Doctor's eyes fixed on Manuel his expression remaining hard as stone.

'OK you guys can carry on your little jape I'll play along, come on, keep it going.'

Frank coughed, 'So how long before you can tell me about the evidence doc?'

Hertz picked up the bags up eying their contents, 'I'll have a full report by tomorrow.'

'Thanks,' Frank turned to leave the medical examiners.

'No problem Frank,' Hertz locked eyes with Lieutenant Montoya, 'stay safe.'

The pair walked down a couple of flights of steps, Manuel was more anxious than a man with a nut allergy eating squirrel shit, 'That was all a joke right, like breaking in the new guy and all that?'

'Yeh the doc's a real practical joker.'

Manuel grabbed Frank by the shoulder, 'Look at me Frank … are they betting on me?'

'How come you're always taking offence kid?'

'People are betting on my life aren't they?'

'Don't worry kid I'm gonna keep you alive.'

'What was that about someone murdering one of your partners?'

'That was last year, Roberts took too many bets, got in over his head and yeh he murdered Alex in his sleep, so the doc holds all the money now, someone makes a bet and the other party has to back it up, cash, beforehand.'

'Maybe I should put a hundred dollars down for two weeks, I mean it's a win, win situation for me.'

'There you go no need to be so glum.'

'That was called sarcasm Frank.'

'Yeh well Alex was in hospital anyway, bullet wound to the head, they were gonna turn him off. Roberts would've been wiped out with all the bets he'd taken so he crept in to unplug him the day before. He got caught by a nurse, but that won't happen again so just relax, remember when the bullets start to fly draw and shoot the bad guys, it doesn't matter if you hit them, just shoot.'

'This is my first day and I'm on the edge of a nervous breakdown.'

Frank smiled, 'You're fitting in already kid,' he glanced at his watch, it was six o'clock, 'time to punch out kid, see you tomorrow and remember stay safe,' Frank winked making his way out of Precinct 17 and back home to his one room apartment.

Frank checked his mail box, made his way upstairs with a bottle of bourbon purchased courtesy of the former Mexican Consulate, shut the door behind him and slumped into his seat. A whiskey tumbler awaited on the desk. A little bourbon and branch water remained at the bottom of the glass, Frank slung the remnants of last night onto his floor; the floor itself obscured by old clothes and empty pizza boxes; Started the stereo, poured bourbon then some branch, reclined to the sound of "I've been everywhere".

'Some day that was, four perps on their way to hell, two murder victims, three dismembered ball sacks, and a game of find and seek in the city sewers. The city's starting to cool down just before it heats up again and Vice come out on patrol to bust pimps, pros and pushers for the rest of the night. Personally I've never understood why people can't be happy with bourbon and Johnny Cash, it's cheaper but then again everything's cheap when you got some high class wetback paying.'

Frank laughed to himself as he tapped his cigarette carton and lit a smoke. 'Yeh, that guy had it all and died on the pan … I wonder why neither of those guys got off the pan. I mean if my balls had been ripped off and the perp had left, why would I stay on the shitter? I doubt the perp waited about making sure they stayed down, so why didn't they run for help, or at least fall over trying? Takes a man a while to bleed to death according to the doc, ah it'll come to me … after a few extra shots and A Boy Named Sue.'

# Chapter Five
## "Cocaine Cowboys"

Frank awoke, a burnt out cigarette dangled from his lips, bourbon half finished, Johnny Cash had stopped playing long ago.

'Damn, what the hell was I thinking about last night, I'm sure I was onto something but ah screw it, where's the bourbon.'

Frank slung a shot down in one go, he rolled his lips back and made a sound of deep satisfaction before grabbing a carton of cigarettes tapping out a morning smoke.

'I guess it's time to write out Williams' report, maybe afterwards I'll find that scrotum's missing owner, he's gotta be looking for it, I know I'd be desperate to get it back! We'll see what the doc's verdict is, it could lead to a break in the case and I can get back to real police work instead of chasing nut sacks like some white trash crack chick with ten kids.'

Frank pulled up in his battered Honda outside Precinct 17, 'Morning Lieutenant, sleep well?' inquired the desk Sergeant.

'Like a baby,' growled a man who could've stumbled up for his morning meal at the church soup kitchen.

Heads turned as they caught a whiff of Frank's bourbon accompanied by dirty ashtray mouth wash, the human embodiment of a public house carpet assaulted their olfactory nerves.

He made his way through the Precinct like a dose of salts after a spicy curry eventually coming to rest at the lab, 'You got anything for me doc?'

Doctor Hertz screwed his face, 'When was the last time you took a shower Frank?'

'Monday.'

'I've exhumed corpses less ... fragrant. You should do something about your personal hygiene.'

'When you give me something to go on I'll take a shower, deal?'

'Well we could both be in luck,' Hertz presented a close up of the unidentified scrotum, 'I've matched the others to their owners, this however has a distinctive marking, a tattoo,' he passed the picture to Frank.

Midgette examined the picture as Manuel entered, 'They said you were up here, got anything?'

He passed the photograph to him.

'His scrotum is tattooed?'

A large bronco adorned the fellow's body part, Manuel drew breath as he considered the pain involved. He came to the quick conclusion that whoever the artist may be he possessed a steady hand.

'Hmm, you recognise it?'

'Yup.'

'And?'

'Cocaine Cowboys.'

Manuel lost some complexion as he lowered the picture, 'The Cocaine Cowboys.'

Frank smirked, 'What's the matter kid you afraid?'

He placed the picture on a nearby table, 'You've got one of their members in questioning?'

'I thought we could take a trip to Warren and Trumbull.'

'Are you crazy that isn't just some drive in it's a BIKER GANG HOUSE, it's the COCAINE COWBOYS' GANG HOUSE. Please tell me you've got backup Frank.'

Frank tapped a smoke from its carton and exited the lab with Manuel in tow, he lit his cigarette whilst walking through a tense office. Frank gave O'Grady a smirk, O'Grady growled across his desk sporting a black eye and glowing crotch.

Frank turned his key in the ignition leaving Precinct 17's parking lot for the Cocaine Cowboys' gang house.

'I've heard of these guys Frank, they're mean, real mean.'

'We're just going for a friendly chat. I'm not looking for trouble kid.'

'But trouble has this way of following you about Frank.'

'How many bullets you got in your pistol?'

'Thirteen and a spare magazine, why don't we stop for breakfast I'm feeling hungry.'

'Take the safety off kid, just in case it gets rough.'

Manuel un-holstered his Glock 41, flicked the safety off then returned it.

'Damn that kid was so nervous his asshole could crush a brick right now. Gotta hand it to him though, even the meanest niggers didn't have the nuts to walk into that place, the Cowboys'd shoot 'em down on sight.'

Frank sang along as Johnny Cash played "Ring of Fire" on the stereo, Manuel began to sweat and the city wasn't even warm … yet.

Frank pulled up outside a diner come gas station come bar, ten Indian motorcycles lined up outside.

They exited the car, the diner entrance swung open ominously like a saloon door in the Wild West. Several bandana clad skulls turned their eyes squinted as two gentlemen entered, sun to their backs.

Frank stepped inside it was guns at dawn, except this wasn't one on one, it was two on eight, that's only taking the men into account, some of those women were rougher than a bear's ass, Manuel was certain they'd pulled a trigger more often than most Mudjahideen.

Frank sat at the bar, a women with large breast dressed in denim and leather approached from the other side, 'Why you here Frank?'

'Is that anyway to greet your ex-husband on a morning?'

A subdued chuckle rippled over the room, she eyed the bikers quickly shutting them up, 'Tell me what you want then get out.'

'Burger and fries for me and my friend.'

She locked eyes with Manuel, 'We don't serve his kind in here.'

'He's with me.'

'What you really here for Frank?'

'I found something yesterday. One of your boys lost his balls.'

'I don't know what you're talking about.'

'I wonder if I searched this place right now what I might find?'

'Nothing,' replied Sally in a stern tone.

Frank stood up, 'Let's test that theory,' Frank produced his badge, 'This is a police search I want everyone here to form a line facing this wall, hands against it.'

Several men rose from their tables hands moved toward holsters, Frank and Manuel's went for their weapons as the jukebox kicked in and W.A.S.P. played "Cocaine Cowboys" at full volume.

Smith and Wesson in both hands Frank fired at the nearest perp ... BANG ... a bandana blew away, the rear of his skull sprayed brains across his compadres. Manuel fired shot after shot not taking a fraction of a second to pause.

'Oh gotta yell, cowboys from hell,

Oh I'm in the Devil's haze,

Oooh I'm on the trail and I'm riding the rails,

Oh, I'm getting blown away!' screamed the lead singer of W.A.S.P competing against bullets as they rang past Frank's ears.

BOOM ... Frank expelled a man's spine onto a W.A.S.P. publicity photograph, four men dressed in glam rock outfits and big hairdos Vertebrae hit the concrete some shattering into goo other pieces ricocheted splattering bikers in spinal fluid and bone whilst still on the draw. Manuel reloaded, pumping bullets one after another like a man possessed.

'I'm gonna -riiide,

Cocaine Cowboys,

I'll be riding high tonight,

Cocaine Cowboys never die!' bashed a high octane metal noise to ripples of gunshots passing from one end of the diner to the other then back again.

A denim clad biker, gang patch on jacket, jumped up with pistol aimed BOOM! His head exploded to the beat of Frank's Model 500, its shell twice the size of a Magnum 44's, blood brains and cerebral fluid detonated in all direction covering tables and chairs.

'Oh I'm gonna ride the range,

High on the plains, high on the reigns,

White lightning lines I'll be,

Riding high, so high!' yelled Blackie Lawless ... BANG ... the music stopped. Sally wielded a smoking shotgun, 'OK PUT YOUR GUNS AWAY!' she glanced at the bikers, 'THAT MEANS YOU TOO!'

Everyone lowered their weapons.

'The man you're looking for his name's Mike, Mike Blair, you happy Frank?'

'I'm still waiting for that burger and fries.'

'Get the fuck outta my bar and take your spic with you, unless you wanna help clean up your mess ... no you never could do that could ya.'

Frank gave a sneer and left the bar/diner, Manuel's heart beat so hard he felt it was trying to rip out of his chest. They got into the old Honda and pulled away.

Frank lit a smoke, Johnny Cash sang, his partner sat in shock, 'You're improving kid, didn't miss a single shot, twenty six bullets in the same perp!' Frank cackled to the sound of "Folsom prison blues".

Manuel turned robotically and whispered, 'You could've got me killed. I heard bullets going past my head.'

'Let's get back to the Precinct, call in that guy's name, maybe they'll have his details by the time we arrive.'

On arrival Mike Blair's file graced Frank's desk, he sat back reading through it, something clicked, Mike Blair and Demetrius Stones served on the same taskforce in Mexico, no link to the former Consulate other than the fact he was in Mexico City the same time.

Frank tapped his keyboard sending an email request for information pertaining to an anti-drug taskforce and Esteban Rivera's employment during the years 2007-2011.

Frank lit up a smoke then poured a shot of bourbon into his coffee whilst considering the conundrum. As far as he could tell no-one went in or out yet somehow, someone, ripped those scrotums off and got away. Neither place had a window large enough that a human being might fit through, in fact the only method of insertion and extraction other than the door was the plumbing … why would you rip off a guy's balls then go into the sewer when you could just flush them. Why would you rip off a guy's balls in the first place?

Frank took a deep drag on his smoke then a swig of his coffee/bourbon cocktail … unless it was the only way to kill the victims. At that moment Manuel burst through the door disturbing Frank's deep thought, 'Hey Frank! Look!'

Frank jumped up in his seat, 'Don't you ever knock?'

'Look, I've got something, two of the victims worked on the same taskforce in Mexico.'

'Yeh, yeh, I sent a request for more information. I've got a question for you.'

'Sure.'

'There are two exits in the Consulates bathroom, name them.'

'Well there's the door.'

'And?'

Manuel's eyes moved around, 'I don't know.'

'The Consulate was sitting on it.'

'The toilet?'

'Right and if I wanted a kill a guy sitting on the pan and the only way in or out is the plumbing what would be his most vulnerable point.'

'There are arteries, I guess his genitals are an obvious target, but how would an individual use the u-bend to assault a man and why?'

'Never mind about motive that'll become clear in time, we need to work out how.'

'There must have been some sort of device in the toilet before he sat down, no it doesn't work out Frank.'

'Why?'

'It'd need to be small enough to traverse the plumbing yet have enough leverage to tear a man's scrotum from his body, that's just not possible.'

'Could have been a rat,' stated Frank.

'A rat, with a nut sack collection? Besides a rat couldn't hold a man on the seat until he bled to death.'

'Whatever it was it had to get a grip on the victim somewhere.'

Manuel shrugged, 'On his scrotum.'

'No, think about it, it rips his nuts off and waits for him to bleed to death, right?'

'Right.'

'Well how does it keep him on the pan while he dies?'

'I guess it'd have to attach itself to his body and have a sturdy anchor, nah this is crazy talk.'

'You got a better theory?'

'They committed suicide.'

Frank took a hard drag on his cigarette burning off a whole centimetre, 'I know you don't believe that.'

'It's the only plausible explanation.'

Frank cackled, 'That guy's got a sweet piece of pussy, a well-paid job, easy hours and kills himself by pulling off his own nut sack?'

'Maybe he got depressed?'

'Fuck me! If that's the case they better put us both on suicide watch! What about Demetrius?'

'PTSD.'

'What?'

'Post Traumatic Stress Disorder, a lot of soldiers coming back have it.'

'How many cases of a man with PTSD ripping off his own nut sack?'

'I don't know.'

'You go and find me one and I'll consider your theory.'

The computer bleeped, Frank clicked on his email, he'd located the third body. Mike Blair was on ice at Wayne County Morgue, fortunately it wasn't too far.


Frank and Manuel pulled up in that old Honda, once inside they were led to Mr Blair; a fresh tag on his toe, heavy stitching from neck to belly button.

'How's it going doc?' Frank offered a cigarette.

The Doctor took the smoke and Frank lit it, 'Another one of yours?'

'Nope just wanted to ask some questions.'

'Well I'm afraid you won't get any answers,' the Doctor was about Frank's height, five foot six and dressed in bloody blue scrubs, 'so what do you want to know?'

'Did you check this perp out?'

'Sure.'

'Notice anything unusual?'

'Apart from his obvious lack of testicles nothing jumps out.'

'Any unusual markings?'

'Other than his tattoos?'

'I mean abrasions, bruises, cuts.'

'I did notice a perforated anal passage as if several fish hooks were inserted under intense pressure.'

Frank glanced at Manuel then back to Doc Maloney, 'Any idea what caused it?'

'None, it didn't kill him but Jesus that had to hurt.'

'So he was alive when the wounds were inflicted?'

'Definitely.'

Manuel observed the corpse lying on a metal bed, 'Excuse me Doctor but why has this man been subject to an autopsy?'

The Doctor froze up and it had nothing to do with the icy temperatures. Manuel locked eyes with Frank then the Doctor yet a reply was not forth coming.

'So did you get the four I sent you a couple of days ago?' stated Midgette.

Maloney removed his gloves, pulled off his scrubs, washed his hands and took out his wallet, 'The spic?'

'The kid's ok.'

Maloney counted off four one hundred dollar bills, 'There you go Frank.'

Midgette placed it inside his wallet, 'Thanks Doc, can you do me some pictures of that guy's asshole then send them over?'

'Sure Frank, anything else?'

'Nah, I'm done for now.'

Doc Maloney made a pistol with his fingers and pointed at Midgette, 'Keep 'em coming Frank.'

The Homicide Detectives returned to the Honda, it was time get back to Precinct 17 and write up the Captain's report.

'What was all that about Frank?'

'What about?'

'The money and keep 'em coming, what did he mean by that?'

'Doc Maloney makes extra cash on the side.'

'How does that work out?'

'You're an inquisitive one.'

'I guess that's why they made me a Detective,' stated Manuel in a sardonic tone.

Frank smiled as the engine chugged into life, 'Maloney helps out sick people.'

'How?'

Frank turned down Johnny Cash as he reversed out, 'Supply and demand economics kid there's people out there who need a new kidney or a new liver and ...'

Manuel put a hand on his forehead then expelled a tired groan, 'Uuuhhhh, he cuts up corpses and sells the organs doesn't he?'

Frank shrugged, 'So what's wrong with that?'

'Oh my God! You send some corpses his way, he gets the organs on ice quick, sells them to the hospital and you, you get a cut from dead perps, right?'

Midgette blew smoke out the car window as dilapidated stores and pawn shops passed by, 'It's supply and demand kid, there's good decent people out there who need a new liver and if they got the cash why shouldn't they be allowed to buy a new one? That's the trouble with this fucking country today, socialism and entitlements, we're more like communists than capitalists!'

'Is that how you justify selling their organs?'

'That's the risk you run when your entire culture is just a fucking death cult worshiping empty sex, guns, drugs, prison and shitty rap music, so deal with it kid ... now you know why I always aim for the head,' Frank cackled as he turned up Johnny Cash, 'besides think about it, some rich white guy's gonna end up with a nigger's heart, you can't say I ain't doing my bit for racial integration in this city!'

'A hundred bucks that's what a man's life goes for these days, assuming all his organs are there and he ain't too screwed up on crack or some other junk. I always thought recycling was a load of bullshit but cold hard cash has a way of changing a man's mind. I gotta keep it quiet, if word got out Al Gore might move in with some sort of cataracts credits scheme ... shifty bastard.

Yeh a man gets a scheme going in this city he's gotta keep his head down, what about Manolito you ask? Bah, I'll cover the kid's ass for 20 days, cash in my four grand then maybe get an extra hundred if his widow donates the corpse.

Hadn't thought of that, I wonder what his wife's like, hmmm yeh maybe I'll take a visit when Manolito's on the long shift, tell her how dangerous the job is down here, how difficult it is for a guy like me to keep her beloved husband safe and how I gotta get some relief or Manolito might not be coming home someday ... heh, heh, heh.'

# Chapter Six
# "Ring Of Fire"

'Time to visit Lebron, that file revealed an interesting link to his past. Damn two faced son of a bitch lied to my face and pulled it off, not many people in this city can do that, not after being a cop for thirty five years. It seems Mr Montel was acquainted with Mr Stones and I'm betting it was no coincidence Stones died in his club that night. My job is to find out what Stones was there for, I'm thinking a drug deal right now possibly smuggling illegals, makes sense with the Mexican Consulate but leaves the biker out the picture.

Nah the way I see it drugs were involved, bigger money The Consulate was probably the Mexican link, let's see what Lebron has to say. The city was boiling like Gordon Ramsay over a half cooked risotto and we pulled up outside Lebron's blues club "The Black Light".'

Frank stepped inside, the band played Muddy Waters in a subdued tone, the bustle and light conversation died as customers observed two Homicide Lieutenants move toward the bar.

Lebron quickly served the gentlemen, 'You trying to tarnish my good name by coming in here?'

Midgette peered around the dingy club, 'Damn, if they closed their eyes your bar would be empty!'

'Keep your voice down cracker,' whispered Lebron, 'now what you want?'

'Could start off with a bourbon and branch for me.'

'Well you'll have to pay this time.'

Frank sneered in the owner's face, 'Is that a fact Corporal Montel?'

Lebron let out a long sigh, the game was up but as to its nature Frank was yet to discover, 'Xavier, one bourbon and branch,' a barman prepared and plonked it in front of Frank.

'Navy SEAL, served ten years in black-ops, two of those in Mexico,' Frank took a slug of bourbon rolling back his lips, 'Ahhhh … according to a report on my desk you served with both Private Stones and Private Blair in the same unit for most of that period.'

'So?'

'So you told me you'd never seen Stones in your life, but what's really interesting is the fact your staff had never seen him in the club before.'

'So?'

'So how come Stones decides to pay his old buddy a visit for the first time since they'd left the military and gets wasted in your club that very night … unless this wasn't the first time you guys had a get together?' Frank emptied his glass and pushed it in the barman's direction, 'Another.'

Lebron was anxious, like Donald Trump at the barbers, you could sense it, 'Maybe I knew the cat, so what?'

'Maybe? You served in the same unit for over a year you numbskull of course you knew him.'

'So what, he came to the club to catch up on old times.'

'Why didn't you tell me Lebron?'

'I couldn't.'

'What about Private Mike Blair?'

'Yeh, sure you know I know him.'

'He's dead too Lebron, died about the same time as Demetrius, got his nuts ripped off.'

Lebron shrugged his shoulders, 'Coincidence.'

'What about Esteban Rivera? And don't lie to me 'cause if I find out I'll fuck your business up permanently!'

Xavier served another bourbon while Manuel took notes, 'OK I knew the cat from back in Mexico.'

'Go on.'

'He worked on the inside, fed us information and shit, that's all, I didn't know he was in the U.S. until you showed me a picture then I realised who it was.'

'Why didn't you tell me all this before?'

'Our operations are classified, I can't go talking shit, identifying folks, even to cops.'

Frank knocked back his second shot, 'Ahhh, I got four people all in the same line of work, same time, same place, killed by the same method except for one. I don't know if you see where this is going but you're kinda looking like the nigger driving a bloody Ford Bronco down the freeway with a piece to his head.'

Lebron poured himself a whiskey, 'Yeh but could that motherfucker play ball.'

'What's the connection?'

'We all served with the 7th, you want more go look in a different place, say Florida?'

43

Frank understood he was stationed at Eglin Air Force Base in Florida, 'I ain't going to Florida without some questions and for that I need answers. So enough bullshit Lebron, if you want this shithole to stay open you're gonna tell me what Stones came here to discuss.'

Lebron drank his whiskey then gestured to the detectives, leading them to his rear office. Once inside and certain they were alone he began to talk, maintaining a nervous demeanour, 'Stones called me the night before, he was scared but wouldn't talk over the phone. He turned up, had a drink, played it cool and while the band played he was gonna come out the shitter and meet me in here.'

'To talk about what?'

'I don't know, that's the truth. I haven't talked to this cat in years and then he gives me a call talking like a crazy man.'

'How do you mean like a crazy man?'

'He's asking if I'm ok, I said I'm fine, then he's asking about other guys in the company, I told him I ain't seen any of those cats for years.'

Frank examined Lebron, he was holding back, as to what was a mystery, as to why there was no question … fear, this guy was terrified. Frank had to threaten him with something far more terrifying in order to coax it out. 'I'm gonna have to close this place for a few months while we sift the crime scene for new evidence.'

'Fine.'

'Maybe I'll let it slip you're paying for police protection.'

'Fine.'

'And you're in business with the Cocaine Cowboys.'

'YOU WANNA GET ME KILLED? THESE NIGGERS'D LYNCH ME!'

'I wanna know what you know Lebron.'

'You're the dirtiest piece of dog shit in this city.'

Frank tapped a smoke from its carton, 'So what did Stones say before he died?'

'He said the guys from our Recon unit were being murdered, he said we were the last and we needed to watch each other's backs. I thought the cat had gone nuts so I fixed him up with some suds and a bitch for the night. Poor bastard gets murdered, tomorrow night and he'd of got some pussy first.'

'You think it was murder?'

'Yeh,' sighed Lebron, 'our unit was infiltrating drug cartels, taking out the top guys first. We used drones to kill those bastards but it was all clandestine you know.'

'What do you mean?'

'We got trained to use drones.'

'OK.'

'No you don't understand these ain't the drones you see on TV taking out children in Pakistan. These things fit into the palm of your hand, move around using bladeless rotors, just a bunch of hoops.'

Frank took a drag then puffed out the smoke, 'How the fuck can that work?'

'Do I look like a scientist bro?'

'You gotta point, go on.'

'I only got basic training, Sergeant King was the main man on drones, it'd enter a mansion through plumbing and ...' the bar owner began to sweat, 'ripped his nut sack off.'

'How did it keep him from running for help?'

'I didn't ask.'

'Fine, do you know where I can find this Sergeant King?'

'Six feet under.'

'So Stones was telling the truth.'

'Yeh, I checked up on the team, looks like I'm next in line Lieutenant.'

'What are you doing about it?'

'My asshole's so tight that if you put the national debt in it Washington'd balance the budget in a heartbeat.'

Frank raised his eyebrows while taking a long drag; he turned to the office en-suite.

'No way bro, I ain't doin' it!'

'I need something, we need something, if I catch one of these drones you keep talking about I got some evidence to back up your story.'

'It ain't no story, it's the truth.'

'And I got a theory,' Frank glanced in Lieutenant Montoya's direction, 'open up the trunk of the car you'll find a pair of bolt cutters,' he chucked a set keys to Manuel.

'Bolt cutters!' yelped Lebron.

Manuel exited the room, 'I've got a theory.'

'Theory?'

'Is there an echo in this room? Yeh I got a theory and I reckon it might just save your ass.'

'You don't get it dude, my nut sack is on the line here and you're talking about using bolt cutters,' he took out a handkerchief and wiped his brow.

That evening Frank and Manuel were on watch in Lebron's bar. Frank was about to test his hypothesis, Lebron was sweating his balls off … so to speak … Manuel was on the phone explaining to his wife why he'd be late.
'Do they do requests?' inquired Midgette.
'Sure, what you got in mind?'
'They know any Johnny Cash?'
Lebron laughed for the first time in days, 'Are you serious? This ain't no honkytonk, it's a blues joint.'
The band stopped playing and Frank called out from the bar, 'Hey you boys know any Johnny Cash?'
The bar erupted in laughter a guitarist chuckled over his mic, 'What you got in mind honky?'
'Personal Jesus.'
He stopped laughing, 'Yeh we know that one honky,' nods were exchanged before he strummed out the song, a pianist played in the background.
The club listened intently, an aura of approval emanated, definitely not the honkytonk expected. Lebron served Frank his usual bourbon and branch water tapping his foot all the while, 'That ain't half bad.'
'Ask them to play Mannish Boy next.'
'Now you're talking the blues.'
'And we can go for a shit.'
After the band finished Lebron had them play Muddy Waters, the three made their way to his office and Lebron sat with pants around ankles staring Frank in the face, 'I can't take a shit with you looking at me man.'
Manuel held the bolt cutters in preparation, as to what he was supposed to do with them he had no idea.
'You're gonna have to look the other way.'
Frank turned his back and lit a smoke, while he puffed away on his favourite brand of cigarette, Camels, Lebron grunted with relief, eliminating days of backed up excrement. It hit the pan with a dull thud in time to the blues. Lebron's brown choo choo train make its way to Mississippi … a pair of glowing eyes illuminated darkness within. Long gangly protrusions glinted below Lebron's nuts, hanging in stillness, he had no idea as it found its mark and in a moment of cold calculated violence struck, 'FRAAANNNNNKKKKK!!!!!!!'

Frank spun to see his bait attempt to flee yet something forced him in place, something evil. Lebron flushed, hitting the handle over and over, Frank pulled him to the side. Manuel poised brandishing bolt cutters not knowing what ghastly sight lurking within the depths might greet his eyes. Lebron lifted one chubby ass cheek whilst screeching like a girl, 'MAKE IT STOP PLEASSSSSEEEE BRO!!!'

What Lieutenant Montoya saw was as confusing as it was horrifying, a winged insect, a metallic mosquito, rested above the waterline. Its wings four static oval hoops, thin shiny legs latched onto the side of the pan secured the beast. From the creature's mouth protruded a pair of pincers, it clasped where Lebron's scrotum met his body ... very, very tightly. From its rear a metallic rod forced its way into a bleeding anal passage, quivering in shades of darkness. The scene was one of demonic violation, Manuel froze in shock observing a metal monstrosity defile Lebron in the most degrading way possible.

'CUT IT OFF BRO! IT'S UP MY ASS!' bellowed Lebron while the band played "Please Have Mercy".

Manuel froze, hypnotized by a demonstration of what evil man was capable of toward his fellow.

'CUT IT OFF KID!' roared Frank as blood mixed excrement squirted out Lebron's trembling butthole.

Manuel pulled out of his coma brandishing a set of cutters with ominous intent, 'JESUS YOU'RE GONNA CUT MY DICK OFF!' yelled Lebron.

'You'll be fine,' grunted Frank into his ear.

'I CAN FEEL HIM ON MY DICK! BRO DON'T DO IT!'

'Calm down I've got the claw,' stated Manuel as he navigated delicately close to Lebron's penis.

'CALM DOWN? I GOT A ROD UP MY ASS, A CLAW ON MY NUT SACK AND BOLT CUTTERS AROUND MY DICK!'

'Your dick's fine,' ... SNAP ... off went the pincers, SNAP, off went the rod and so Lebron tipped onto the floor jerking in pain.

Frank made for the pan rather than assist Lebron, he wanted whatever that evil construction was, it retract its legs from the porcelain and descend into a mixture of shit, blood and piss. Without hesitation Frank plunged his hand deep ... KEERRRPLUNK!

He was in up to his elbow, damn, it smelt peperoni pizza, extra olives with a dose of hot urine, not too bad considering some of the places Frank frequented in the past. If it weren't for the toilet water he could probably make a good guess as to what type of cheese. That turd was darn resilient though, bobbing up and down like a dolphin splashing in and out of the water. Each time it came up for air it dispensed a dose of Domino's or was it Papa John's? Yeh Papa John's, Frank couldn't mistake their garlic sauce, it always made him retch.

'GNNAAAHHH!' Frank gagged as he took hold and retrieved the drone. Midgette stood up drone in hand and the remnants of Lebron's last few meals slipping from his jacket sleeve towards the floor. He bashed the drone against a wall until it no longer function, like a dying mythological beast its eyes went dead and body fell loose, 'Fuck me I need a drink!' Manuel smiled, 'Nice job Frank.'

Lebron squealed like a pig, 'CAN SOMEONE CALL AN AMBULANCE!'

At that moment Xavier opened the door investigating screams he'd detected whilst at the bar. His boss lay on the floor fumbling his genitals with a bloody metallic rod protruding from his behind. Frank held a strange device, dripping with excrement. The other guy was sweating like an animal, clenching a pair of bolt cutters, 'Errmmm did I come at the wrong time?'

'Xavier, call a damn ambulance,' shouted Lebron.

'Are you sure?'

'Jesus Christ! Call the fucking ambulance you dumb nigger!'

'Yes sir,' Xavier exited the room.

'Can you get up?' stated Frank.

'I can't, it's this thing up my ass, I can't stand up.'

Frank peered at the mosquito like creature in his hand, 'Well we know how, next we find out who.'

'How?' inquired Manuel.

'We wait.'

'Why?'

'The owner of this thing's gonna want it back, I don't think it'll be too long before he turns up, until he does I reckon he'll forget about you Lebron.'

Lebron lay face down on the toilet floor, 'Gee thanks.'

'Damn that guy's ass stunk, it's the sauce I'm sure, I got nothing against Pappa John's but someone needs to tell them their sauce tastes like nasty pussy. After it's been through Lebron's asshole it smells nearly as nasty as it did going in the other end.

More than thirty years solving crime and I'm reduced to this, Hawaii Five-O was never this way, I watched that show when I was a kid and all I wanted to be was a cop. Steve McGarrett ran around an island full of babes in bikinis, permanent sunshine, surfing, high profile cases. When McGarrett said "Book 'em" you knew justice had been done for another week and he was headed to the beach until another case turned up. I joined up and what did I get? A shithole in Detroit full of niggers, spics and white trash, no cooling breeze on a sunny day just boiling heat in a concrete jungle, dodging bullets to the sound of a rap beat instead of canoeing in salt spray to the Hawaii Five-O theme tune.'

# Chapter Seven
## "I Want To Break Free"

'Driving home, Manolito's off to see his wife, I gotta buy some soap, washing powder and crap like that, even I have standards. There's no way I can turn up with Lebron's processed Papa Johns all over me. I got nothing against Pappa John's pizza it's just the sauce tastes like an Amazonian tribesman's foot and that's before you eat it; in fact when it comes out Lebron's asshole it don't smell so skanky.
Anyway, I'll stop off at the mall, get some soap and powder to wash these clothes, I'll be a new man come morning. Did I say the city was hot? Sorry, it gets to me, but I gotta say it's so damn hot the Taliban'd be wearing Bermuda shorts and a vest.'

Frank cruised into town parking his car in the underground lot below a multi-story shopping mall. He made his way to the elevator, a family waited, sniffed, looked at each other then turned to see its source waiting behind.
The bell rang and doors opened, he waited yet the couple and their two children stepped aside, 'You take this one,' stated the husband.
Frank moved past into the elevator, 'Mommy, that man smells like doggy doo,' noted a seven year old girl.
'Shhh,' said the lady placing hands upon the child's shoulder then locking eyes with Midgette as the elevator doors closed.
The doors opened to the mall, he hated these places but there's nowhere left to shop. Floors of sanitised stores with standardised human beings oozing insincerity, there were more unpaid college loans behind counters than meth heads in a trailer park.

He made his way to the nearest store, after entering Frank shuffled to an aisle, whilst searching for powder and soap a young lady browsed the opposite aisle. Dressed in a pair of cycling shorts and a T-shirt she bent over to check the lower shelf. Frank couldn't help himself, as she bent down his attention was dragged from product hunting to ever thinning fabric stretching further than Obama at a press conference. Everything was on show captivating Frank's sad mind in a leering moment, he watched it ride up her behind and examined the resulting camel toe thanks to a packet of lentils, strategically placed on the bottom shelf of the aisle.

Suddenly she snapped up, deciding against those lentils for whatever reason.

Frank remained frozen, 'Jesus Christ.'

She turned to witness Frank peering at her personal area until he too snapped out of it yet it was too late.

'HEEEELLLLPPPPP!'

'Hey lady it's fine,' he said reaching out towards an Asian woman.

She fixed her eyes on a pair of stinking excrement and blood stained arms trying to grab her, 'HEEELLLLPPP ME HE'S GOING TO KILL ME!' screamed the woman in her early twenties.

'No, you don't understand I just saw your ass and … , I mean I'm here to protect you.'

'HEEEELLLLPPP POLICE!' she started hurling shopping from her basket in Frank's direction.

He realised she was terrified by his bloody arms, 'Please listen to me, it's not like that. I had to pull a metal rod out a guy's asshole today …'

'POLICE, POLICE, HELP ME!'

A mall cop entered the aisle just as Frank finished his sentence, 'I held him down, my partner cut it out with a pair of bolt cutters, but that's another story,' the mall cop shouted, 'HALT! RAISE YOUR HANDS!'

Frank turned around to see some overweight guy in a uniform with a cap, 'Who the fuck are you?'

'Mall security.'

The young lady ran past Frank and stood beside the mall cop, 'This man's a sexual pervert and a rapist!'

'Fuck you bitch!' stated Frank in an incredulous tone.

'It's ok lady, I heard what he said,' the mall cop pointed his night stick, 'Now put your arms up pervert!'

Lieutenant Midgette walked slowly towards the cop, as he advanced the cop retreated with club stretched between them. They left the aisle and ended up just inside the store near a register. Shoppers outside stopped to rubber neck the situation.

'You've got no authority to arrest me asshole, I'm a cop,' Frank produced his badge.

'You can buy those on the internet!'

He put his badge away to produce a Smith & Wesson Model 500, 'You can't buy these on the internet fat boy.'

Observers screamed diving for cover, the Asian lady screamed again, the mall cop gulped before a fart reminiscent of a dying rat making its last squeak exited his rear.

'Now all I want is some soap and something to clean these clothes then I'll leave, ok?'

'DROP IT ASSHOLE!'

Frank glanced to his left, the store owner had a sawn off shotgun aimed right at him.

'Put down gun or I shoot!' stated the man in an East Asian accent.

'Back stabbing slanty eyed bastard!'

'YOU HEAR ME? DROP IT OR YOU DIE ASSHOLE!' he was very agitated, there was no point in any blood shed so Frank put his piece down.

The owner peered at the mall cop now standing in a puddle of piss, 'Call police, I watch him.'

The mall cop couldn't control his bowels let alone call the police, instead the young lady made a 911 call.

'You think you rob my store? I put plenty GI in ground Tay bastard!'

On being referred to as "Tay" he realised this man was Vietnamese, Frank's father served in the Marines during the Vietnam War, he'd heard that reference once or twice.

'If there's one thing I hate more than niggers its communists.'

The old man laughed, 'Maybe I am Ho Chi Min? Maybe I waste your ass before cops come? Give bullshit story to cops they believe me not dirty shit like you!'

The mall cop let another rat squeak slip out, grabbing everyone's attention, next the police turned up brandishing pistols. Four men aimed at Frank whilst one shouted instructions, 'Lay on the ground with arms above your head!'

Frank kneeled then lay face down.

'Put your arms behind your back!'

The Lieutenant complied, 'Hey my name is Lieutenant Frank Midgette you'll find my badge inside my jacket.'

'Don't talk unless I ask a question!'

'What's your name boy?'

'I said shut up punk,' the officer kicked Frank in the ribs.

A man in blue picked up Frank's weapon whilst another went through his pockets, 'Gary, take a look at this.'

The officer in charge lowered his pistol to observe the badge while Frank was being cuffed, 'Precinct 17 huh? I hear that place is a real shithole, that's if this is real.'

'Now let me outta these cuffs,' grumbled Frank.

'Officer, put this perp in the wagon, book him for sexual assault with a deadly weapon, impersonating a police detective and stinking like a dead dog in summer time.'

'Yes sir,' they dragged him to his feet and out the mall.

'Ray, take this lady's statement, I'll get the store owner.'

'Yes sir.'

The cops wrapped up their business taking statements and comforting the young lady still recovering from what she believed to be a stalker or some kind of sex pervert.

Frank was piled out of the van and into Precinct 13 for booking. Dragged up to the desk Sergeant, he reeled in disgust at Frank's powerful odour, 'Name?'

'Kiss my ass!'

A police officer dropped Frank's wallet on the desk, 'Thanks Gary, now let me see what I can see ... Frank Midget?'

'That's Midg-ay it's French!'

The Sergeant smiled, 'Whatever, we've got a nice warm cell waiting for you Mr Midget you'll probably recognise some of your old friends.'

As they led Frank to his cell Gonzalez was walking down the corridor, 'HEY GONZALEZ!'

The Lieutenant noticed Frank being man handled to the jail cells. One of the police officers stopped and addressed the Homicide Lieutenant, 'Do you know this man sir?'

Gonzalez let off a sneer, 'I've never seen this man before officer, what's he in for?'

'We just booked him for sexual assault and impersonating a police detective.'

'Put him in with Roberto.'

The policemen chuckled, 'Yes sir.'

Frank was tosses into a cell, the thick metal door and peep hole slid shut. He sat down on the bed, a scream from beneath the covers made him jump in the air. From under the sheets a strange man ascended, short curly black hair, a Freddie Mercury moustache, skin tight leather strides, boots and a bright yellow jacket, 'Hi stranger, my name's Roberto.'

'Where'd you get a name like that kid?'

'My Father was Italian.'

'Really?'

'Oh yes,' the young man strutted towards Frank as Frank moved backwards, 'There's no need to be frightened … what's your name honey?'

'Frank, my name's Frank.'

'Frank in Detroit and Ernest in New Orleans?'

'Yeh, I guess so.'

'What are you in here for Frank?'

'A heap of shit that's what.'

Roberto looked at the blood and human waste staining Frank's Jacket, 'Looks like you've been having fun, say why don't you slip out of that dirty jacket?'

'I'll keep it on if you don't mind.'

'You can have mine if you're chilly … wouldn't want those nipples getting hard, would we?'

Frank placed his hands on his pockets searching for something.

'What you looking for?'

'Ah they took my smokes.'

Roberto opened his jacket to produce a carton of cigarettes and a book of matches, 'I've got some smokes.'

'You mind sharing?'

Roberto smirked, an evil naughty boy smirk which sent a shiver down Frank's spine, 'Sure, I'll give you a smoke Frank the best smoke you've ever had in your life cowboy.'

'Don't do that kid.'

'Come on honey we've got the whole night together.'

Frank banged on the cell door, 'HEY OPEN THIS DOOR!'

The peep hole slid open, 'What's up?'

'This guy's a psycho you can't leave me in here!'

A laugh echoed on the other side, 'Twenty bucks says he can't walk in a straight line tomorrow morning.'

'I'll take that bet,' echoed another man on watch before the peep hole slid shut.

'Do you want to break free Frank?'

Frank viewed a flesh crawling grin hang below Roberto's moustache. He'd witnessed many a frightening thing from gun fights to car crashes, this guy had to be in the top five, 'Stay back kid.'

'I want to break free from your lies, you're so self-satisfied I don't need you, I've got to break free Frank!' sang Roberto as he eyed Frank's crotch.

'I'm warning you kid!'

'Don't deny your true feelings Frank, release yourself from the shackles society places on us, embrace that which is beautiful, love, from one man to another. I want you to break free, will you break free with me Frank?'

Midgette swung his boot straight into Roberto's groin,

'GNNNAAAAHHHHH!' the young fellow dropped to the floor like a stone in a lake.

'How's that for breaking free kid?'

Roberto rolled on the cold floor clutching his nuts as he wept like a girl, 'Why Frank, why?'

'Pain is so close to pleasure.'

'This don't feel good Frank.'

Midgette sat down on the single bed provided for two occupants, he went for his cigarettes only to remember they'd been confiscated at the desk. Looking down Roberto's smokes had been discarded due to a throbbing pain between his legs. Frank bent down, took the smokes and book of matches, tapped the carton then struck a match ... damn that was a good smoke. He burned a centimetre off before thanking his cell mate. After relaxing for a few minutes he leant against the cell wall, 'So what you in here for Roberto?'

Roberto sat on the opposite side of the cell, back against the wall, 'My father used to beat me!'

'Sounds like the kinda guy I'd get along with.'

'He thought I wasn't tough enough, not manly like my brother.'

'What you IN FOR Roberto?'

'I'm not in for anything, I can leave whenever I want; my brother's the Captain of this Precinct.'

'Sure,' Frank chuckled then offered Roberto a cigarette, 'smoke?'

'I'm trying to give them up.'

'One won't hurt ya kid.'

Roberto leant over tentatively.

'Don't panic kid I ain't gonna hurt you, just don't pull any of that Freddie Mercury shit again and we'll get on fine.'

'Roberto smiled and took a cigarette while Frank lit a match, 'Thanks.'

'How the hell did you get these smokes past the guards?' Frank thought for a moment then looked at his cigarette in an odd way.

'Don't worry I didn't hide them up my ass, it's like I said my brother's the Captain, he lets me stay here. What's your story, how did you end up in here?'

He let out a sigh accompanied by a ball of smoke, 'Ah, a misunderstanding at the mall, some woman thought I was a pervert ...'

'I know what you mean,' interjected Roberto.

'Well I get arrested and try to tell them I'm a fucking cop but they don't listen. Then I see Gonzalez after I've been booked and he says he's never seen me before.'

'Why would he do that?'

Frank took another deep drag, 'Ah it was all to do with the time he caught his wife cheating on him. He organised this off hours sting ... turns out I was the guy she was banging, heh.'

Roberto giggled.

'Yeah well it's like I'm paying for his wife's sins ever since, I mean that bitch has had more paternity tests than three fucking seasons of Maury. She fucked her way through more than one Precinct but I'm the guy responsible.'

Roberto's eyes stopped as he concentrated, he put the pieces together, 'Are you that Midget guy he's always bitching about?'

'The name's Midg-ay and yeh I guess so.'

Roberto pulled and expression of delight, 'Gonzalez he's such an asshole you know.'

'You're preaching to the choir kid.'

'So if you're really a cop why don't you just show them your badge like Columbo?'

'Looks like they took some gook's word for it, bastards refuse to check my badge.'

'I could tell my brother.'

Frank gave him a condescending look, 'Sure you could.'

Roberto stood up and tapped the door, 'OH HELLO, GUARD IT'S ME.'

The peep hole slid back, 'What you want Roberto?'

'I want to speak with my Brother.'

'He's busy.'

'Tell him,' Roberto turned to Frank, 'What's your rank?'

'Lieutenant, homicide, Precinct 17.'

'Tell him Lieutenant Frank Midgette from Precinct 17 is being held inside one of his cells.'

'Sure.'

'And get me another packet of cigarettes and some matches.'

'Anything else?'

Roberto turned to Frank again, 'A bottle of Stag.'

'A bottle of Stag and two glasses.'

'I can't authorise that, no alcohol is allowed in the cells.'

Roberto began to weep, 'All I wanted was a drink with my friend but he wouldn't let me, no Brian you don't have to fire him just send him to personnel or something like that ...'

'OK, OK I'll get the damn liquor,' the peep hole shut and within thirty minutes Frank and Roberto were drinking away.

'So here I am in a cell drowning my sorrows with a cross between Hannibal Lecter and Freddie Mercury. All we need is some music and it'd beat most evenings with my ex-wife, that's for sure.

The kid knows a lot about this Precinct, must be a regular visitor, these bastards have it so easy. Paid a fortune to police easy street, what kinda bullshit is that?

I guess the Captain'll be notified in the morning, until then I'll make sure I sleep on my back ... after Roberto here has dropped off.'

# Chapter Eight
## "Highwayman"

'Friday morning, I got a hangover and a psychotic queer staring back at me. Darn these jail beds are hard, feels like I slept on a plank of wood with my head nailed to it. Where's that bourbon, that'll wake me up … ahh!' Frank tapped his cigarette carton and lit a smoke, 'Yesterday was a crazy day, went from cutting a metal rod out Lebron's ass to some nip bitch throwing lentils at me to sharing a cell with Freddie Mercury's mentally disturbed twin brother.

I know I say it often but damn the city's heating up, by afternoon if someone farts in here it'd be a cool breeze.'

The peep hole slid back, 'Frank Midget?'
'That's Midg-ay.'
The door pulled back grinding to a halt alongside the wall, 'Good news Lieutenant you're released.'
He gave Roberto one last glance, 'See ya later kid.'
'Bye, bye, bye Frank,' waved Roberto.
The Lieutenant followed the guard, twenty bucks exchanged hands, upon reaching the desk Captain Jane Williams displayed a matronly stare whilst clutching a case file. A man in a suit stood alongside her, they chatted, something about him was familiar; Frank couldn't quite put his finger on it.
'Your Lieutenant, Captain Williams?'
'Thankyou Captain Pane, it won't happen again.'
Frank pointed at the Precinct Captain, 'Do you know a guy called Roberto?'
The middle aged man with dark short curly hair replied in an awkward tone, 'I see you had the company of my brother, Roberto, last night.'
'What's he in for?'
'Roberto isn't charged with anything Lieutenant he just likes the company, besides it's safer if he's inside the Precinct.'
Frank dragged a palm down his face, 'For him or the public?'

'Goodbye Captain Pane,' stated Williams before strutting into sunshine wearing a black pencil skirt, white blouse, jacket and shades. Once inside Frank's car she handed him the keys along with his effects, 'Drive Frank.'

'Where to?'

'Your apartment.'

A seedy expression honed in on a pair of knees poking out from Williams' pencil skirt.

Williams grimaced, 'I just ate Frank.'

'OK what're we going to my place for?'

'Do you expect to turn up at the Precinct dressed like that?'

'Fine,' he started the engine and pulled away checking his glove compartment for last night's evidence, it was still there.

Williams opened a brown folder, 'Sexual assault of a female inside Phan's Family Store.'

'That's bullshit.'

'According to her statement you ogled her as she viewed goods on a lower shelf. She was alerted to a man's presence upon hearing the words "Jesus Christ" behind her. Next a man in a blood and urine stained jacket, smelling of faeces grabbed her rear.'

'That's a lie.'

'She states that after molesting her, the perpetrator said "That's fine" then went on to state "I saw your ass and had to put a metal rod in it". The mall cop says he heard the perpetrator state, "Something about being his partner and cutting the victim up with a pair of bolt cutters". The perpetrator shouted "Fuck you bitch" as the victim fled,' Williams closed the file and let out a long sigh.

Frank lit a cigarette, lowered the window and blew a puff of smoke, 'You don't believe that heap of shit do you?'

'Strange as it seems I don't.'

'The store owner pulled a sawn off on me too, back stabbing bastard, December the sixth nineteen forty one, don't think we've forgot.'

'December the seventh.'

'What?'

'Pearl Harbour was December the seventh Frank and just so you know they're both Vietnamese.'

He took a long drag on his cigarette, 'I guess that's two villages those Air Force bastards missed. Bunch of Harvard rich kids such bad shots it's hard to understand how they manage to procreate!'

'You're lucky she didn't press charges Frank.'

'Why didn't she if I'm such a dirty pervert?'

'Two reason, first off I told Captain Pane the last time Lieutenant Midgette felt a piece of ass the toilet paper broke on him. Secondly the store camera shows quite clearly you didn't touch the woman, in fact she assaulted you.'

'Damn right,' Frank cackled as he blew smoke out the Honda, 'I tell you something else that dirty bitch bent over so far I could see what she ate for breakfast, shit I could almost smell it through those shorts!'

Williams placed a hand on her stomach with an ill expression, 'I get the picture Frank.'

'What about the mall cop?'

'We thanked him for his diligence, gave him a pat on the back and he walked away. So tell me what happened yesterday that caused you to be filthier than usual?'

Frank pulled the drone from his glove box, 'This,' Williams reached out to take the item, 'I pulled it out a nigger's ass last night, got shit and blood all over me,' Williams retracted her hand to cover her nose and mouth.

'What is it Frank?'

'A murder weapon.'

'Why isn't it logged at the Precinct?'

'The owner's gonna want it back and if it's logged in at the Precinct it'll be too easy to recover.'

'I don't understand.'

'I have a suspicion the murderer isn't a criminal gang or organization, I need to keep it out the Precinct to test my theory.'

The battered Honda drove past tall buildings of steel and glass, up market consumer hives moved along dying off sharply into what might have been a post-apocalyptic movie set, burnt out houses, trailer parks, streets controlled by drug dealers in the day and pimps at night, Frank pulled up to his apartment block.

The Captain had to step outside, clearing her lungs foul smog where an atmosphere usually existed. After choking a little she pulled out a handkerchief, its perfumed cloth provided a barrier between her senses and rotting pizza in a sea of unwashed clothes sprinkled with bourbon and assorted trash.

'There's nothing out there Jane, come on in.'

She entered the hell hole watching where she stepped and what she stepped on.

Frank was going through clothes on his floor, sniffing underwear until he'd selected a pair of shorts, shirts, trousers, a tie, socks and a jacket came next.

'What the hell are you doing Frank?'

'Picking out my clothes, can't wear this to work can I.'

'Frank those clothes are dirty.'

'But some are dirtier than others.'

'I'm feeling sick Frank.'

'Sit down, take it easy,' he gestured towards his chair alongside a work desk.

Frank went into the shower and washed off yesterday's filth. While Frank scrubbed himself down she examined the unwashed sheets on his bed, Williams noticed an old takeaway box and groaned, they'd gone out of business two years ago!

Frank walked out of the shower naked, 'Jesus Christ Frank put some fucking clothes on!'

He grabbed the least dirty pair of boxer shorts laid out on his bed with the rest of today's apparel, 'Come on Jane I'm sure you've seen worse.'

Williams looked away from Frank, 'I'm afraid I've never been a Coroner.'

'Funny.'

'So tell me about this case.'

'I thought it was meant to just keep me busy until I consent to be put out to pasture.'

'Oh come on, you're the best detective in that Precinct.'

Frank buttoned up his shirt whilst giving her a smug grin.

'Don't get too full of yourself.'

He reached for a tie, 'It's going fine, Manolito's working out, he might be a good cop one day.'

'If he makes it.'

'Yeh, I hear you had him down for ten days.'

'I hear you've been betting through the doc, is it true?'

'Who told you that?'

'So it is true.'

Frank put his socks on and tied his shoelaces, 'Let's get outta here.'

They got back into Frank's old Honda and headed to Precinct 17. Rush hour was dying down as people reached one of their many part time jobs thanks to Obama care and the State's shitty handling of anything economic.

Williams took a sigh of relief, the carbon monoxide atmosphere of a Detroit city morning was comforting compared to Frank's hovel.

Traffic dissipated quicker than usual, so quick she became struck by desolation on the road; in fact they were the only occupants on this strip of road. Despite driving through a residential area traffic was non-existent save Frank's Honda and a black truck rather reminiscent of a S.W.A.T vehicle.

'Frank ...'

'I see it, you packing?'

'Sure.'

'Then get ready, you know what to do.

Williams put down her paper work and checked her firearm, a Brown Hi-Power 9 mm with a thirteen round magazine.

Frank eyed her weapon, 'You still carry that thing?'

'This pistol killed more perps than every damn electric chair in this country, besides it was my Grand Father's.'

'Yeh and before that the SS-Officer he shot.'

She flicked off the safety and pushed the pin back, loading the chamber, 'Some brought back fine art, gold, jewels ... he got a pistol, but life's a bitch Frank you know that better than anyone.'

The truck with black glossy paint and blacked out windows pushed in front then turned to block the road, men piled out in military uniform, four altogether. They held automatic rifles, not M16's, something smaller, Frank didn't know what model but they were definitely not standard military issue.

'I guess they want to speak with us,' stated Williams in an ominous tone.

Frank bought his Honda to a stop.

'EXIT THE VEHICLE!' bellowed a man dressed in black combat fatigues. Frank opened the door.

'EXIT THE VEHICLE WITH HANDS ABOVE YOUR HEAD, WHERE I CAN SEE THEM!'

Both cops exited the Honda hands raised, 'My name is Captain Jane Williams of Precinct 17, please identify yourself.'

'SHUT UP AND FOLLOW INSTRUCTIONS! PLACE YOU HANDS ON THE HOOD OF THE VEHICLE!'

Frank sneered at the young man, 'Fuck you.'

'PUT YOUR HANDS ON THE HOOD OF THE VEHICLE, IF YOU REFUSE I AM AUTHORISED TO USE DEADLY FORCE.'

'I refuse.'

The kid became agitated, 'PUT YOUR HANDS ON THE HOOD OF THE VEHICLE, NOW!'

Williams looked back and forth between the kid in fatigues and Frank, she didn't know why but they were still alive ... Frank had called his bluff.

'You ain't gonna shoot me kid, you want that drone too bad, don't you?'

'PUT YOUR HANDS ON THE VEHICLE, THIS IS YOUR FINAL WARNING I WILL NOT ASK YOU AGAIN!'

Frank glanced at Williams, he had that look in his eye the look that after ten years on the beat she recognised all too well, the devil was coming to breakfast.

Frank's hand moved inside his jacket, 'I'm a Police Officer, here's my badge see for yourself.'

She moved her hand to her belt.

'DON'T MOVE OR I WILL USE DEADLY FORCE!'

Midgette and Williams drew like a pair of gunslingers in the old west whilst Johnny Cash and June Carter sang "Jackson" on his car stereo ... BAM, BAM ... they fired in concert. Frank's target lost his head, detonating gore over comrades as June Carter sang, 'We got married in a fever, hotter than a pepper sprout.'

Williams put three rounds into her boy, two in the chest and one in the head, her father's pistol as reliable as the day it was issued.

The cops dropped behind the Honda's open doors as a stream of burst fire ripped out. Frank grinned across the inside of his vehicle, she shook her head as bullets smashed through the window and rattled inside the door whilst Johnny Cash sang the chorus.

'SURRENDER YOURSELVES NOW!' bellowed one of the young men.

Frank chuckled, dropped onto the floor, aimed ... BAM ... the kid lost his leg from the knee down, his limb bounced off the truck coming to rest about twenty feet from its former owner now screaming to his comrade for assistance.

'WARTENBERG AND MURRAY BOTH DOWN, KAUFMAN IS INJURED REQUEST PERMISSION TO WITHDRAW!' screamed a desperate man into his mic.

The doors to the van opened, two men exited armed with pistols, Williams hit the deck ... BAM ... some guy's knee escaped out the back of his leg dropping him to the ground so he might join his friends' pity party.

'When I breeze into that city, people gonna stoop and bow,

All them women gonna make me, teach 'em what they don't know how,' sang Johnny Cash.

BAM ... off flew a leg spinning in the air, a rotor blade spraying blood over the area ... BAM, BAM, BAM ... another fell, Williams putting extra rounds into his body for insurance.

'But they'll laugh at you in Jackson, and I'll be dancing on a pony keg,
They'll lead you 'round town like a scalded hound,
With your tail tucked between your legs,
You're going to Jackson, you big-talkin' man,
And I'll be waitin' in Jackson, behind my JAYPAN FAN!' sang June Carter accompanied by groaning men bleeding onto a Detroit freeway on a warm summer's morning.

Frank stood up, a man raised his pistol ... BAM ... his body convulsed, jumping off the floor for a second to a Smith & Wesson Model 500 cannon.

Williams rose, a boy tried to aim his rifle with one hand ... BAM, BAM, BAM ... she fired, both hands firmly gripping her family heirloom, the lad's arm dropped, head rolled to the side, eyes gazed into the abyss, the last thing he heard was Johnny Cash and June Carter ... not a bad way to go thought Frank.

Two remained on the ground, one too wounded to resist the other on his back empty hands in the air, 'We got married in a fever, hotter than a pepper sprout,
We been talkin' 'bout Jackson, ever since the fire went out,' the song ended in a puddle of blood and a jigsaw of limbs.

'Call it in Frank.'

Frank approached the driver now surrendering himself, he pulled his pistol on the man, 'Who sent you kid?'

'I'm only permitted to divulge my name rank and number,' groaned the prisoner.

'Where the fuck do you think you are kid, Afghanistan? You're gonna tell me who your boss is and why he sent you here,' he aimed at the young man's privates then cocked the hammer, 'or you can say goodbye to Richard and his friends.'

'OK, OK, DON'T SHOOT!'

'YOUR BOSS NOW OR YOU'LL BE SINGIN' SO HIGH THEY'LL HAVE TO DIVERT AIR TRAFFIC!'

'COLONEL VINCENT GRAHAM.'

'WHY YOU HERE KID?'

'RECOVERY, WE'RE HERE TO RECOVER A DRONE.'

Frank released the hammer and lowered his weapon, 'So this Colonel Graham he's in charge?'

'Yes.'

An ambulance and several squad cars arrived at the scene sirens blaring. 'Tell your boss that if he wants his drone he can come and get it himself. I don't do business with gofers ... I kill gofers for fun, understand kid?'

The young man nodded his head as medics swarmed around him, placing him into a gurney before raising him inside the ambulance.

'Some start to the day but I don't compromise in case you didn't know. Assholes that want to do business at the end of the gun are gonna take a down payment in lead and if they're lucky receive the rest from a catheter,' Frank took a drag on his cigarette.

'I've been pounding dirty sidewalks since before those kids were an itch in their daddy's bag,' Frank chuckled to himself, 'most of the gang bangers I see every day could out shoot those Florida boys. I hear it's a nice state too, good food, good drink, clear seas and rich old ladies paying young Cuban landscape gardeners overtime ... nah I'll stick to retiring in Hawaii.'

He exhaled smoke as bodies were collected and Williams gave a statement, 'The city's smoking hot, like Joan of Arc's panties at an English barbecue, I gotta get back to the office and switch that air conditioner on, then wait for this asshole in Florida to visit.'

# Chapter Nine
# "Rusty Cage"

'Nice and cool in the office, feels especially good when some other asshole's paying for it, in my apartment I sweat into the mattress all night. Manolito smelt like a whores panties, the kid wears so much cologne it makes my eyes water. He's busy writing up yesterday's report, word for word, nice to see dedication to procedure, I'll soon knock that outta him, heh.

I'm just waiting, waiting for the owner of this drone in my desk to show his face, his boys' corpses disappeared from the morgue and no media turned up on the freeway. It confirms Lebron's story, when Colonel Graham turns up I might make some real cash for a change. They spend two trillion on fighting sand niggers and my air conditioner has needed a service since Vietnam, made in America.'

Lieutenant Montoya entered the room with a brown paper file in hand, 'Lieutenant Midgette, everything's written up if you could have a look I'd be grateful.'
Midgette lit up a smoke as he glanced over the file, 'Looks fine.'
'I'd appreciate it if you read everything, in case I made any mistakes.'
'Don't worry about it Manolito I trust your work, and you can call me Frank.'
'By the way I looked up Manolito last night.'
Frank grinned as he closed the file, 'Yeh, you watch the show?'
'My wife did.'
'And?'
'She said it was a typical white male orientated TV show pandering to negative racial stereotypes.'
Smoke and laughter burst from Frank in concert, 'What do you think?'
Lieutenant Montoya sat down, 'I think I need some tequila before we go after those evil comancheros!'
'That's my boy,' he pulled out a flask, 'bourbon do?'
Lieutenant Montoya accepted the flask and took a swig of bourbon before handing it back to Frank.

'My wife bitched all night about equality and racial harassment and how I need to report you, all I wanted was a night's sleep.'

Midgette tapped his smoke increasing a pyramid of ash, 'Got a picture of her?'

Montoya opened his wallet displaying a family photograph of his wife and daughter.

'Ooh nice catch kid, I wouldn't mind seeing her ass bounce up and down on my belly.'

Montoya retrieved his wallet, 'Classy Frank.'

'Come on kid, it's the closest I get to any these days.'

'Apart from that woman you molested last night.'

Midgette fixed his eyes on Montoya, 'Who told you about that?'

'It's all over the Precinct, so did you molest that woman?'

'Of course not, that fucking bitch was crazy, sure she caught me by surprise but Jesus Christ her whole fucking rig was on display for everyone to see. I just happened to be the only person there and hey I'm guilty for liking pussy, somehow that makes you a pervert in this day and age but if I'm getting married to another man and adopting a kid from a Romanian orphanage the President gives me a fucking medal!'

'OK Frank, calm down, just don't be surprised if O'Grady mentions it.'

'Ahh fuck it, I take comfort in knowing that when she's as old as me she'll be BEGGING for a guy to grab her skanky old rig in a grocery store, heh, heh, pompous bitch, she'll be crying into her noodle soup that dirty old perverts won't give her a second look,' he took a long drag and blew the smoke up into a vortex created by a grinding old air conditioner, groaning under the strain of the office temperature.

'What's next with the case Frank?'

He removed the damaged drone from his draw, 'Let them come to us.'

'You think they'll come here for that?'

'I'm betting if this little drone became public it'd cost the military more than just dollars.'

'Oh?'

'There's skeletons in closets and this is the key, think about it, as far as we know it's been used to murder drug lords, but what if they wanted someone else dead?'

'I don't understand Frank, what does it matter if they kill a drug lord or a terrorist or any enemy of the state?'

'Well Mr Obama was good enough to pass a law permitting extrajudicial executions of U.S. citizens … so what if that enemy of the state happened to be an American citizen living in the U.S.?'

'You're not suggesting that thing is used for state sanctioned executions?'

'Why not?'

'How the hell do you get from assassination of drug lords to some conspiracy theory involving state executions, besides what about due process?'

'You're joking kid, since when did anyone give a shit about due process?'

'No Frank you need …'

'Did Osama Bin Laden get due process?'

'But he was a terrorist that murdered …'

'Ah, ah, ah, allegedly murdered and since there was no due process we'll never know for sure, just a state execution while Obama and Hilary watched their favourite snuff movie together at the tax payers' expense, right?'

'You're crazy Frank, you believe all that conspiracy bullshit?'

'No, but I know there was no due process and what about all those poor bastards in Gitmo?'

'Well, I guess some of them …'

'Name one!'

'Well I can't off the top of my head!'

'Drones in Pakistan, what about all the innocent Pakistani's murdered by drones?'

'That's a mistake.'

'Tell me kid would that fly in a court anywhere in this country?'

Manuel fell silent taking a deep frustrated breath.

'You're a cop, if you murdered an innocent and said 'I'm sorry judge but I thought the five year old child and his Mother were evil terrorists' your ass wouldn't touch the ground until it hit the nearest penitentiary!'

'OK so what's your point Frank?'

He raised the drone, 'This gets past things like the media and if they got caught the State has a safety net enshrined in law, and we know they've been carrying out extrajudicial killings of veterans already.'

'Suspect, it's just another theory, remember due process Frank?'

'When was the last time you took a shit kid?'

Manuel chuckled for a moment, 'Good point Frank.'

'Exactly, these bastards are playing dirty and don't want to be discovered, as long as we have this drone we're gonna stay alive.'

'What happens when they come for it then?'

'I don't know, but one thing's for sure, if he goes back to Florida with this,' he held the metallic mosquito up above his head, 'we're paying a visit to the morgue … as residents.'

Manuel gulped, 'I think I need another drink.'

Frank opened a draw and pulled out a pair of glass tumblers, placing them on the table he then produced a bottle of bourbon, pouring a drink he leaned back and took a slug, 'Aahhh,' grunted Midgette as he rolled back his lips, 'damn this is good stuff.'

Captain Williams entered the office unannounced, 'Jesus Christ you've got him drinking on the job too!'

Lieutenant Montoya was lost for words so Frank replied in Manuel's absence, 'Take it easy Jane, he's got bigger things to worry about.'

'Like?'

'Have you heard anything from high up, any unusual requests maybe from Florida?'

'No, why?'

'The shit's gonna hit the fan.'

'You mean it didn't already?'

'Sure, but it's gonna continue until the owner of this,' he put the drone on his desk, 'gets it back into his possession.'

'What do you mean the shit has hit the fan?' asked Montoya.

'Today on the freeway, we got jacked by some soldiers.'

'Really?'

'You mean it hasn't even been reported?'

'Not that I know of.'

Williams locked eyes with Midgette, 'I saw four squad cars, that incident has to be filed somewhere.'

A fire alarm rang out in the Precinct, Midgette and Williams figured something wasn't quite right. She pulled out her Browning Hi-Power, loaded it and flicked off the safety. Frank pulled out his Smith & Wesson Model 500 and cocked the hammer. Manuel knocked back some liquor before drawing his Glock 41, loading the chamber and flicking off the safety.

Midgette placed the drone in his desk draw, 'I've got a bad feeling about this.'

'Shit has this way of following you around,' stated Williams lowering her voice.

'Maybe so,' said Manuel, 'but my money's on Frank,' he smiled and the others smiled back.

Dark figures in combat helmets could be viewed cautiously moving in, holding rifles, searching offices, they approached Frank's office. The atmosphere was tense, Manuel's lungs felt so tight he couldn't pass oxygen through, his heart beat like a drum, in fact he wondered why the others couldn't hear it.

Frank raised his weapon and as four or five converged on his door … BAM … the glass collapsed to blood and bone spraying in all directions … BAM, BAM, BAM … Williams and Montoya let rip as men's souls were dragged down to hell by the devil himself, those remaining hit the deck of their own accord.

Men screamed their last pitiful moments, others called out orders taking up tactical positions. Frank grabbed Montoya by the collar and hit the deck as did Williams, the RAT-A-TAT-TAT of automatic fire blew pictures and awards off the walls. Had Montoya been standing he'd have joined those souls holidaying in Villa Satan.

Rifle bursts ceased and a voice called out, 'MIDGET! DO YOU HEAR ME MIDGET?'

Frank didn't answer, only placing a finger over his lips, making certain Montoya did likewise.

'MIDGET! I'M HERE FOR THE DRONE, THAT'S IT. THROW THE DRONE OUT AND I'M GONE, UNDERSTOOD?'

Williams peered at Frank with an expression of desperation. Frank crept silently onto his knees to pull an item off his desk … a bottle of bourbon. He then tore Manuel's shirt sleeve off dousing it in alcohol. Next he stuffed the bottle shut with the cloth, lit it and chucked it out the broken window where the demands had emanated … WOOSSHHH …

'AAAHHHHHHHHHH!!!'

Frank nodded, Williams replied in kind, they leapt to their feet, Montoya followed just behind. Standing at three broken sheets of smoky glass the cops aimed and fired … BAM, BAM, BAM, BAM, BAM. Eight men laid dead, one on fire, Frank exited his decimated office and stood over a man trying to remove his combat armour before roasting alive.

Several staff including O'Grady heard gunfire and were entering the office with weapons drawn, aghast at such destruction, they watched silently as Frank raised his pistol aiming at the desperate soldier's head, 'And just so you know, the name's Midg-ay … it's French,' … BAM! The soldier stopped moving, his body smouldering, a bullet hole dead between his eyes.

'Captain are you OK?' blurted O'Grady surveying a tale of death and disaster chronicling the last minute.

Williams holstered her Browning, 'Thank God you got here O'Grady.'

His expression betrayed a confused state of mind.

She sneered, 'Someone's gotta clean this shit up!'

Frank walked up to O'Grady and cocked the hammer, there were screams from female office workers, O'Grady froze at the sight of Frank's cannon which shifted to point back at Frank's office ... BOOM ... he put a bullet into the old air conditioner, 'About time they replaced that piece of shit!'

A whirring came from the roof, Frank ran up the steps as sprinklers rained down extinguishing a corpse in the open office area. On the roof a Blackhawk helicopter lifted off, an older man in a beret stared into his eyes until they could no longer distinguish one another.

He checked the roof for further threats then reloaded his revolver, perhaps they'd try means other than violence in future. Returning to his office medics examined the bodies alongside police officers taking statements , 'Lieutenant Midget can I have your witness statement please?'

'Sure, they came from the roof and I got two of them.'

'Did you see them on the roof?'

'Yeh, just now they took off.'

'But you didn't see them enter from the roof.'

'I was in my office, I heard a fire alarm, after everyone evacuated the building these dark figures are searching the office.'

'Through the office glass?'

'Yup.'

'Did they open fire on you first?'

'Sure they fired on us and we returned fire.'

Lieutenant Montoya was shocked, his expression didn't hide the fact. Frank peered at the detective and gave a slight nod, Montoya turned to his Captain only to receive the same ominous nod.

'Are you certain they fired first sir?'

'As certain as the stink on my first shit this morning kid!'

'What happened next?'

'We returned fire, dropped a couple, they had us pinned in my office so I took a bottle of bourbon left over from last year's Christmas party and made a Molotov cocktail, threw it in as a distraction, we moved to the shattered windows and shot it out with them.'

71

The police officer peered up from his notes, 'Fortunate there was a bottle of bourbon in your office, would it be usual to find liquor in your place of work Lieutenant?'

'Are you trying to imply something kid?'

'Of course not sir, please continue.'

'Well that's it, we finished them off, I went to the roof and their chopper was lifting off.'

'Could you identify the helicopter sir?'

'It was big and black with rotor blades,' replied Frank in a sardonic tone much to his workmate's amusement.

'No, did you recognise the make or model or perhaps any insignia on the helicopter, was it military or civilian?'

'Military, maybe a Blackhawk but I don't know.'

'Good, did they say anything or make any requests?'

Frank tapped his cigarette carton, put a smoke in his mouth, offered one to the officer taking his statement but he declined. Frank lit up his smoke, took a long drag, 'They said nothing kid.'

'Do you have any idea why they might have come here?'

'No idea kid.'

'Are you certain Lieutenant?'

'Jesus Christ, for all I know they were transporting Hilary's dirty panties to the laundry!' another ripple of murmured chuckles could be detected.

'Fine,' he presented Frank with a clipboard and pen, 'read the statement then if your happy with it please sign it.'

Frank signed the statement, walked into his office, sat down, opened his draw before remembering he'd used the bourbon as a firebomb. He pulled out a few glasses and produced his hip flask pouring out three drinks. Everyone looked on almost evangelically, fixated on his drinks, 'AIN'T YOU ASSHOLES GOT WORK TO DO?'

Precinct staff began to make themselves busy picking up furniture and putting paperwork back in order.

Frank put his feet on the desk as he knocked back the drink and puffed on his cigarette.

'Lieutenant, be careful not to set the sprinkler off again,' advised an office girl in her late teens early twenties.

Frank grinned, 'Don't worry kid,' he gestured with his bourbon glass to the sprinkler directly above, 'that thing hasn't worked since I moved in here.'

She scanned his office and it hit her, his was the only dry area, he must have disabled the alarm and cut the fire suppression system off in his office for obvious reasons.

Frank put his glass on the desk and grabbed his crotch, 'But there's still one sprinkler that works like a charm.'

The office girl cringed at the man. Williams looked up from taking her statement, 'Frank, you've got as much class as a soiled leopard skin mankini.'

'You know me Captain,' he shifted his body slightly and broke wind, 'dog's gotta eat.'

Williams glanced over at the disgusted office girl, 'Now you know why Frank gets his own office.'


'Stupid bastards tried to steal the drone, might of even worked if I hadn't disabled that sprinkler years ago. I reckon there must be a tracking device in this thing, the most I know about tracking is from episodes of Star Trek when the guy sporting metal boomerang glasses was talking to the computer guy that was super intelligent but still hadn't worked out how to use contractions. How is that? He's a genius but talks like a retard and is a social cripple, come to think about it that sounds like every single President since Kennedy!

Anyway what the fuck was I talking about? Ah right tracking, well aside from techno jabber about transponders on Star Trek I've got no idea, so either I destroy it and they hunt me down anyway or ride the storm until they turn up to do a deal.

A lot of men have died for that piece of metal so far, it's gotta be worth a few bucks, who knows maybe I could retire to Hawaii and spend my days drinking martinis on the beach with Steve McGarret while babes in bikinis fight over who's gonna wake up with me tomorrow? Either that or I get a permanent retirement and go to meet Roy Orbison six foot under, bah, life sucks, time to listen to Johnny Cash, drink a bourbon and branch, smoke a cigarette and wait, I have a feeling they'll be here to take possession of their body bags.'

# Chapter Ten
## "I Want To Be Loved"

'So here I am, drinking, smoking, listening to Johnny Cash while the Precinct gets cleaned up. The end of this case is coming, I can feel it, like a credit card statement you don't want to arrive. It hits the carpet at your wife's feet, next thing you're in Guantanamo, she's red faced and screeching about a subscription to "BurningHotTeenBitches.com" and all you can do is apologise instead of telling her that after twenty years of marriage and an extra seventy five pounds, fifteen bucks a month is a small price compared to the plastic surgery she'd need!
Anyway, what the hell was I talking about again? Ah yeh, I can feel it in my gut, they're coming. Hopefully we'll be doing business like civilized human beings.
I was gonna say the city's hot, but with those sprinklers going off and no air con I gotta say it really is the humidity that gets you, you know, like trying to breath in a lift full of people when Chris Christie farts just after leaving a Tex-Mex all you can eat!'

Staff cleared up Precinct 17, fire crews departed, bodies bagged and tagged, Frank remained at his desk.
Distant first but slowly it grew until the noise of a chopper filled the room. Staff looked upwards, someone important had landed, hands moved to pistols.
An army uniform appeared at the bottom of the staircase, he surveyed total devastation caused by the last shoot out, 'I'm looking for Midget, Frank Midget.'
Eyes shifted towards Frank's office, he took their direction and strolled through blood stains, puddles of water and burn marks.
Frank heard a knock on his door, 'Come in.'
A man who hadn't slept for at least one night closed the door behind him, before either could speak the Captain shouted, 'Clear the office, everyone get out until I call you back!'
After a minute of shuffling Williams entered the room to offer her hand, 'Captain Jane Williams,' they shook hands, 'and you are?'
'Colonel Victor Graham, Fort Eglin.'

'Why are you here Colonel?'

'You've been killing my men Captain.'

'Don't send anymore and they'll live longer.'

'I'm afraid it's not that easy.'

'No?'

'You have something I need to recover.'

Frank took pleasure watching him squirm, he took another slug of bourbon and rolled back his lips as it hit the back of his throat,

'AAAHHHH,'

The Colonel peered at a man slumped over a leather seat, 'I assume you are Frank Midget.'

'That's Midg-ay you ignorant piece of dog shit.'

'My apologies Mr Midgette.'

Frank poured himself another drink.

The Colonel turned back to Williams, 'Do you usually permit your men to drink on duty?'

'Just Frank.'

Midgette had a twinkle in his eye then raised his glass toward Graham.

'So what do you want Colonel?'

Frank opened a desk draw and chucked a plastic bag on his desk, inside were the remains of what Colonel Graham sought. The Colonel moved toward it until Frank drew his pistol, 'Ah, ah, ah, Colonel, not so fast,' he cocked the hammer, the Colonel halted.

'Frank, put that away!' demanded Williams.

'Forget it Jane, if he gets that drone we're both dead.'

'You can't shoot a Colonel, put it away.'

'I'll blow this asshole away if he gets any closer.'

'What do you want Midget?'

'The truth Colonel.'

Graham narrowed his eyes on Midgette, 'It's simple, the war against drugs has changed since we were kids. It's all about hacking servers, implanting tracking devices and drone warfare.

A bright spark came up with a Helmholtz cavity propulsion system.'

Frank furrowed his brow.

'Don't ask me, I'm not paid to understand that kind of crap, what it boils down to is a drone capable of travelling through water and air.

So we put it to use, terrorising cartels for the last couple of years. Those bastards are so scared constipation has reached epidemic proportions in some areas of Mexico,' the Colonel laughed.

'I know that, but how come you're killing your own people?'

'Security, we can't have the truth getting out. Those backward Mexicans are so superstitious they believe the Devil's punishing them for their sins. If they discovered the nature of Project Deadpan it would be a disaster for the war on drugs.'

'Bullshit, the war on drugs is already a disaster, we both know that … I spent time researching your activities south of the border Colonel,' he put down his drink and pulled out a carton of cigarettes, 'smoke?'

'No thankyou I'm giving it up.'

'Fine,' he tapped the carton on the desk, picked out a cigarette, 'You see I got pals who work in the industry.'

'Industry?' Colonel Graham frowned, 'What the hell are you talking about, you don't know anyone involved in this war.'

'But I do Colonel, I'm very close to the biggest dealers and distributors in Detroit,' he had that twinkle in his eye, 'do we understand each other Colonel?'

Colonel Graham turned to Williams, 'I have no idea what this man is talking about Captain, now order him to release my drone and I'll be out of your lives forever.'

Williams didn't trust the Colonel, she was certain he'd get his drone then waste them at the first opportunity, 'What are you talking about Frank?'

'The Colonel here, he has his own racket, right Colonel.'

'ANOTHER WORD MIDGET AND …'

Frank raised his weapon aiming dead between the Colonel's eyes, 'The name is Midg-ay,' he burnt a centimetre off his smoke, 'The Colonel has his own cocaine distribution network, supplied by a single Mexican cartel which coincidently remains un-hit by Project Deadpan … right Colonel.'

'I have no idea what you're talking about.'

'Maybe I should get on the blower to the General at Fort Eglin? Ask him what you're doing here, ask him why his men have been getting wasted on the streets of Detroit? And how come his Colonel running Project Deadpan has a bank account in the Cayman Islands.'

'You're bluffing Midget, I know men like you, all talk and no substance.'

Frank pulled a phone from his pocket, 'I got General Cronin on speed dial, wanna play call my bluff?'

Frank put it on speaker phone then hit speed dial, it rang ominously, Williams, Graham and Midget glanced at one another.

Someone answered, 'Hello who the fuck is this, damn these infernal devices, CAN YA HEAR ME?'

Colonel Graham recognised the voice, nearly shitting his pants he lurched for the phone but Frank raised his weapon.

'Okay,' whispered Graham, 'just turn it off!'

'IS THAT YOU GRAHAM? HOW THE HELL DID YOU GET THIS NUMBER? GRAHAM? GRAHAM? DAMN THESE MACHINES, IS IT ON? MARTHA IS THIS THING WORKING PROPERLY?'

Midgette cut the line, 'So the full story Colonel.'

'Fine, you're right, why the hell not? The damn military sends bags of cash to sand niggers and what do I get? No pay raise and a pension half those cave dwellers are laughing at and all for putting my ass and my boys' asses on the line so some corporation can sell weapons that don't even work!'

'So you decided to sell drugs to Americans,' stated Williams.

'Don't be so high and mighty Captain, I know what you and Midget are involved in, protection rackets, extortion, illegal sale of body parts.'

She fixed her gaze on Frank, 'I thought that was over!'

The Colonel spoke in a frustrated tone, 'Look that's all superfluous, suffice to say no-one is innocent ... so what do you want for the drone?'

'First I want you to know I have everything on file, and it'll hit the General's and a few others desks if I pass away by means other than natural causes ... on a yacht getting blown by supermodels,' he coughed whilst trying to laugh.

Williams rolled her eyes, Graham nodded his head, 'I understand Mr Midget, so I'll ask again, what is it you want?'

Frank put away his phone then lowered his pistol, 'A Saddam.'

Silenced purveyed, dripping water was all that could be heard.

'Are you crazy? That's a whole $750,000 ... IN CASH! I don't just have that lying about you know.'

'What's up, you boys ran out of briefcases?'

'Damn you Midget,' the Colonel's hand moved toward his pocket, Williams went for her weapon, 'I have to make the call.'

She relaxed and he called in, 'This is Colonel Graham, I need a Saddam asap,' he listened for a while then replied, 'Yes I repeat I need a Saddam, what is your ETA ... excellent Colonel Graham over and out,' he grimaced at Frank, 'Your money will be here in twenty minutes Midget.'

Williams coughed politely.

'What's your price Captain?'

She went into her purse, wrote something down on a piece of paper before passing it to Graham, 'You can send the same to this account.'

He examined her details before glancing upward, 'Cayman Islands?'

She raised her eyebrows.

'You people are dirty bastards. I've come across drug lords with higher ethics, you know that?'

Twenty minutes later and a second chopper could be heard, a young man trotted down the staircase with a zipped carryall bag. He saluted the Colonel now having a tipple with his new found comrades. Graham returned the salute, took possession of the bag and dismissed his soldier. As the chopper took off he opened the bag to produce a brown leather briefcase. Frank took possession, opened it and grinned like a kid on Christmas day, $750,000 sat before him in used bills, 'Sweet.'

'Satisfied?'

'Like I took my first shit in a month Colonel.'

Graham held out his hand, 'The drone?'

Frank placed it in his palm, 'Don't try and stab me in the back Colonel. If you have my file, you'll know what happened to every fucker who tried.'

'I understand Mr Midget,' Colonel Graham took the bag.

As Colonel Graham walked back to his chopper Frank shouted, 'And that's Midg-ay, it's French.'

The Colonel flashed one last sneer before departing, shortly afterwards a chopper could be heard lifting off.

Williams let out a sigh of relief, 'Whooo that was tense!'

'Drink?'

'No thanks ... and Frank.'

'Yeh?'

'You and the doc have been cutting me out on the organ deal?'

'You got an account in the Cayman Islands?'

'Let's just call it even.'

Frank closed his briefcase, 'I'll take some time off if you don't mind.'

'Sure, see you tomorrow?'

He nodded his head, case in hand, cigarette in mouth.


That evening there was a knock on Manuel's door, 'Will you get that?' asked his wife.

Manuel stopped playing with his daughter walked into the hall, opened the door and there stood Frank Midgette, 'What the hell are you doing here?'

'I came to visit my partner, what else?'

'Look this isn't a good time ...'

Frank barged his way in, 'Nice digs.'

'Yeh I'm still paying for it, look Frank maybe another time.'

'Manuel, who is it?'

Frank followed the sound of her voice into the lounge as she exited the kitchen, 'Give him some money for a meal then send him out Manuel, quickly,' she moved toward her daughter holding the five year old tightly.

'He's not homeless, he's my partner. Frank this is my wife Victoria, Victoria this is my partner, Frank Midgette.'

Frank offered a hand, she glared pulling her daughter away. Frank looked around and moved toward the couch, 'NO KEEP AWAY FROM THAT!'

'What?'

'I'll bring out a chair from the dining room,' Victoria passed her daughter to Manuel then retrieved a wooden chair, 'Sit here Mr Midgette.'

He sat down and pulled a carton of cigarettes out.

'There is no smoking in this house Mr Midgette,' snapped Victoria. She accosted Manuel into the kitchen, 'What's he doing here, my Mother's visiting!'

Manuel spoke under his breath, 'I didn't know he was coming.'

'It's Sonia's birthday, I will not have my Mother in the same house as that filthy man.'

'Maybe he could use the shower?'

'I only cleaned that shower today, look at him, he looks and smells like a wino.'

'I'll get rid of him, don't worry,' Manuel moved into the lounge, 'Look you've gotta go, it's my daughter's birthday and her Grandmother is visiting.'

Frank's eye twinkled again, 'She as hot as her daughter?'

'I gotta ask you to leave.'

'Fine, but let me give Sonia her present.'

Manuel's five year old girl ran up to Frank despite Victoria's best efforts, 'Where's my present?' asked an excited Sonia.

'Right here.'

'I'm sorry Mr Midgette but I refuse to accept anything purchased with your dirty money,' a holier than thou pitch suited her raised nose along with platted hair and matronly clothes.

Frank pulled a leaflet with receipt attached and handed it over to Manuel, he examined it for twenty seconds then spoke to his wife, 'I think we should consider this Victoria.'

'Never, I will not touch it.'

'Mommy, can I see it?'

She held her daughter back, 'No Sonia.'

'Why mommy?'

'The wages of sin is death!'

Manuel pushed it, she wouldn't accept the paperwork so he held it before her eyes. After ten seconds Victoria snatched Frank's offering, an education at the best private school in Michigan, bought and paid for by Frank for Sonia Montoya.

After reading about the excellent facilities and the long list of accomplished persons who'd previously graduated she peered at Frank, 'I'll consider it ... thank you ... would you like to join us for supper?'

'Sounds good to me.'

'What did I get for my birthday?' cried Sonia.

'Don't worry,' said Frank, 'Come here, you wanna see my badge?'

The doorbell rang, Manuel and Victoria rushed to greet the Mother in law. After taking her coat Manuel escorted her into the lounge. Mrs Martinez stepped inside to see her granddaughter on Frank's knee ... holding a Model 500 Smith & Wesson, 'OH MY GOD, CALL THE POLICE!'

Manuel rushed in, 'Frank, what the hell are you doing?'

'Uncle Frank was showing me his gun.' protested the young girl as Manuel picked his daughter off Frank's knee.

'Uncle? I had no idea you had a brother Manuel,' she looked Frank up and down in a disparaging manner. She pulled a handkerchief from her pocket to cover her nose.

'He's my partner, at work.'

'Why does he smell like a dead coyote?'

Frank stood up offering his hand, she refused to shake it, 'I had a rough day at work Miss ...?'

'Mrs Martinez, have you heard of a shower Mr ...?'

'Midgette, yeh but I've been busy, if I knew you'd be here I'd have cleaned up,' Frank winked at the lady.

'Supper is ready Mother,' smiled Victoria.

Her Mother put a hand over her stomach, 'Sit me away from Manuel's workmate and I might keep it in.'

'Love to see a lady that tries,' winked Frank.

'Frank, shut up,' Manuel stuck an elbow in Frank's side. He chuckled in his Mother in law's direction, 'I have to apologise, you know at the Precinct women have a name for Frank.'

'They do?' inquired Midgette.

Trying to ease tensions Manuel continued, 'They call him the man no deodorant can tame!'

Neither Victoria nor her Mother laughed, Sonia frowned and asked, 'What does that mean?'

'Why is Mr Midgette here Victoria, I was told it would only be us.'

'He brought Sonia a present for her birthday Mother.'

'Oh how nice, do you have to buy the ammunition separately or can my Granddaughter maim herself now while I watch?'

Victoria produced the leaflet from her piny, two waves crashed upon the shore of Mrs Martinez's face, one of surprise then elation. Mrs Martinez quickly took a hold of herself and fired off that same stern glare Victoria displayed earlier, there was no doubt where it came from.

Mrs Martinez approached Frank with hand out, they shook hands, she leant in to whispered in his ear, 'If you're yanking my chain Mr Midgette I'll have your balls for breakfast,' she leant out and spoke so everyone could hear, 'Why thank you Mr Midgette, I'd be honoured if you would join us for supper.'


'Damn that was the first decent meal I've had in ages but Jesus it's caused a lot of gas, no wonder those spics smell funny.

The only thing as hot as the food was Manuel's wife, give her some time to come around and I'll be knocking the bottom outta that ass while he's on a double shift, heh. As for the Mother in law, well I guess she didn't connect with my sense of humour, when we said our farewells, I asked her to say hello to Roy Orbison when she gets home, heh, well I thought it was funny.

Sonia got her trust fund, sure changed his wife's attitude and besides what was I gonna spend the money on? Better she gets a good start in life than blowin' it on hookers and Johnnie Walker.

So here I am alone again, sitting in my apartment listening to Johnny Cash, drinking bourbon, cleaning my pistol and creating enough gas to crash the oil market for the next decade.

Another case closed, seems the small guys always end up in prison or a body bag while the head honcho cashes in, maybe the little guy'll win next time. I'll head on down to Lebron's this weekend, let him know the Colonel's agreed to leave his nuts attached, if I'm lucky I'll get laid. Did I say the city was hot?'

# The End

Printed in Great Britain
by Amazon

41182780R00046